Guarding Shakespeare

Shakespeare

A Noir Novella

Quintin Peterson

ℚℙ Ram Press

Guarding Shakespeare

Library of Congress Control Number: 2013904706

ISBN: 978-0-9891369-0-7

Cover Design by Quintin Peterson. Puck sculpture by Brenda Putnam (1890 – 1975); Photo by Theodor Horydczak (1923 – 1959), taken ca. 1934: Courtesy Julie Ainsworth, Head of the Folger Shakespeare Memorial Library's Department of Photography and Digital Imaging.

Printed in the U.S.A.

 **Ram Press**

Washington, D.C.

For Luther Wayne Chaney

Shakespeare Sonnet 72

O lest the world should task you to recite
What merit lived in me that you should love
After my death, dear love, forget me quite,
For you in me can nothing worthy prove;
Unless you would devise some virtuous lie,
To do more for me than mine own desert,
And hang more praise upon deceasèd I
Than niggard truth would willingly impart.
O lest your true love may seem false in this,
That you for love speak well of me untrue,
My name be buried where my body is,
And live no more to shame nor me nor you.
For I am shamed by that which I bring forth,
And so should you, to love things nothing worth.

August 20th, 8:31 P.M.

Destroyed by the Great fire of London in 1666, St. Mary Aldermanbury Church, which had stood since the 12th Century, was rebuilt in Portland stone by Sir Christopher Wren, but was demolished again in 1940 by the Blitz, the sustained strategic bombing of Great Britain by Nazi Germany between 7 September 1940 and 10 May 1941. London was bombed by the Luftwaffe for 76 consecutive nights and more than one million London houses were destroyed or damaged, and more than 20,000 civilians lost their lives.

Buried in the remnants of its churchyard, in the twice scorched earth of this twice blighted hallowed ground, are the remains of Henry Condell and John Heminge, key figures in the production of the First Folio of *Mr. William Shakespeares Comedies, Histories, & Tragedies*, which was published in 1623. The two had been partners with the Bard in the Globe and Blackfriars theatres.

In the footprint of the church are bushes and trees and gardens. In one of the gardens, in the old graveyard of the church, there is a monument to Henry Condell and John Heminge, crowned with a bust of William Shakespeare.

Before the monument to Condell and Heminge, two well-dressed Englishmen draped in London Fog trench coats stood in the dark, in the pouring rain under black umbrellas. The hair of the older of the two was silver and the younger was graying at the temples. When they required confidential, face-to-face communications, this had been their clandestine rendezvous point for years.

The older of the two glared at the bust of Shakespeare.

He slammed a fist against his thigh and muttered, "Damn it! Damn it all to hell!"

"It was acquired a week before we tracked it to its last owner," the younger man explained.

"Where is it now?" the silver-haired man demanded.

The younger man swallowed hard and said, "It was acquired by...the Folger Shakespeare Library."

"Bloody hell!" cursed the older man. "There are only 232 First Folios known to exist and the Folger Library has 82 of them. England has only 8. But that isn't good enough, no; the Folger has to acquire everything! Early Modern books, manuscripts, artwork, *everything*!"

The older man paused and inhaled deeply to calm himself before he continued. "Just how the hell am I supposed to acquire it now?"

The younger man replied, "We'll just have to steal it."

"Rubbish," the older man retorted. "You bloody well know that some places are impenetrable. Such places that immediately come to my mind are the Vatican, Fort Knox, and the Folger Shakespeare Library."

"With all due respect, sir, I don't believe so," the younger man disagreed. "I can assure you, *anyplace* can be penetrated, it's just got to be an inside job. I'll put someone in place there immediately to scout for a likely candidate among the staff."

The older man nodded and said, "Very Well." He sighed and without looking at his protégé continued, "Over the past twenty years, I've gone to considerable expense and devoted an inordinate amount of my precious time to locate and acquire this treasure and I will not be denied. Get it. Money is no object. But certainly by any means necessary."

The younger man nodded. "Just leave it to me, sir. I will acquire it."

The silver-haired man turned and looked the graying man in the eye. "See to it, Mr. Whyte."

"I will, Mr. Johnson."

Mr. Johnson turned on his heel and briskly strode away toward his waiting limousine, leaving Mr. Whyte standing there in the torrential downpour.

After a few moments, Mr. Whyte turned his gaze to the bust of William Shakespeare and stared at it for a time. He removed a cellular phone from a pocket of his trench coat, scrolled through the phone book, and speed-dialed the selected number. After a moment, he spoke into the phone.

"I need your help once again, my dear. This time, the job is in America."

[0000]

HALLOWEEN, 2104 HOURS

On Capitol Hill in the District of Columbia, on the 200 block of East Capitol Street, SE, adjacent to the John Adams and Thomas Jefferson buildings of the Library of Congress, near the United States Supreme Court, and one block up from the United States Capitol, stands industrialist Henry Clay Folger's gift to the American people, the neoclassical Folger Shakespeare Memorial Library, majestic and mysterious, a city unto itself; a shining city on a hill.

Clad in Georgia white marble quarried from Stone Mountain, the Folger is often misidentified by tourists and other passersby as one of the Library of Congress' buildings. Indeed, the Art Deco masterpiece is in perfect harmony with the architecture of the federal buildings that surround it. However, the treasure trove of rare and priceless English Renaissance books, manuscripts and objects d'art, which includes the largest collection of Shakespeare First Folios and Shakespeareana in the world, is not a public building, but a private research library for vetted scholars from around the globe.

On the west and east ends of the building are the library's two glass and cast aluminum double front doors that match the grilles over the tall windows above the bas-reliefs. The winged horse Pegasus is carved on the planters on either side of the staircase to these doors. Masks of Comedy and Tragedy are displayed above these doors, Tragedy on the east side, Comedy on the west.

No one knew the building better than disgruntled employee Special Police Officer (SPO) Lt. Norman Blalock; he'd been guarding the library for 25 years. That's why he was the perfect candidate to pull off an inside job and heist a priceless artifact from the venerable institution's underground bank vault.

Passed over for promotion again, most recently six

weeks earlier when he'd been informed that the position of captain, second in command, was being given to new hire Nathan Rockford, a retired DC police officer; and further disheartened when Chief Malcolm Leonard had also suggested in the same breath that it was time Norm started thinking about retirement, had been hard for Norman to swallow. To make the prospect of retirement more palatable, Norman had decided to accept a generous counteroffer:

He was going to steal a priceless artifact from the library's vault that night and retire a very wealthy man shortly thereafter. In fact, he was in close proximity to the treasure now…

Lt. Blalock, clean-shaven, tall, dark, and trim, wearing a fresh uniform consisting of navy blue slacks riding just right on the tops of spit-shined combat boots, a heavily starched white shirt choked by a navy blue necktie, and a navy blue commando sweater bearing on each sleeve blue, yellow and white circular Folger Shakespeare Library Police shoulder patches embroidered with Shakespeare's family crest and a shiny gold metal badge and matching name tag on either side of its half-bust circumference, was hiding in the storage/elevator service room on the Gamma Deck of the Folger's underground complex, evading detection by a fellow officer with a K-9 conducting a random interior security sweep.

Norman Blalock wiped sweat from his brow with his left palm and struggled to control his rapid breathing as he fretted about getting caught. He'd had to do some finagling to execute his scheme, to come this far, and it would be a crying shame if he failed after all the work he'd put into this caper…

Norman had volunteered not only to cover Sergeant Gary Thomas's 1400 – 2200 hours shift when Thomas took annual leave that day, but to be Fire Watch Officer as well. During the run of the Folger's current production of Othello, the Folger's fire alarm system had to be deactivated during each performance due to the play's smoke special effect using haze. Haze registers as smoke to the system's smoke detectors, causing a false fire alarm and the initiation of the water fire suppression system in the theatre, which would drive the patrons from the building soaking wet and terrified. Therefore, a guard had to be assigned to Fire Watch, to visually inspect every part of the building at regular intervals, giving him or her license to wander the building at will. The Fire Watch Officer would also be on Water Watch in the art vault that evening to keep an eye on a damaged water pipe there that had been temporarily repaired while the building engineer awaited delivery of a replacement part to affect a permanent repair…

A scant few minutes before he'd had to hide from the K-9 officer, he'd advised SPO Cary, who was manning the Guard's Desk aka Central located in the west lobby, that he was going to conduct a fire watch. SPO Cary then had reminded him to check the art vault for leaks, unwittingly giving the heist his Good-Seal-of-Approval.

"Sure thing, Luther," Norman had told him.

Norman had casually said hello to his co-conspirator, exotic beauty Kavitha Netram, who was sitting in the Gift Shop, and she'd casually said hi. He then had ran up the three steps leading to the west wing of the Authorized Personnel Only section of the Folger and proceeded down the hall to the elevator on his left. He'd pressed the call button and the doors opened immediately. He'd walked into the elevator and pressed 3. If the elevator records were pulled, they would confirm that someone, that *he*, had used the elevator to go to the top floor at that time. Also, Luther would assume he had, as usual, started his Fire Watch on the top floor of the west wing.

On the third floor, he'd gotten off, turned right, and ran down the stairs to the basement.

Stealthily, making sure not to make the wooden stairs creak, he'd silently made his way up the stairs as quickly as possible.

On the first floor, he'd taken a peek to make sure no one was watching, turned left and tiptoed to the door to the Registrar's Office, quietly opened it, and silently closed the door behind him. He'd pushed through a set of double wood and glass doors and stepped into the Gail Paster Reading Room, formerly known as the Old Reading Room. Blalock then had proceeded across the room, through the half-door next to the Librarian's Desk, and through a wooden door leading to a stairwell. Keys in hand, he'd run down three flights of carpeted stairs to Gamma Deck, unlocked a metal door, and slowly opened it. He'd looked around the space on the other side of the door to make sure that he was alone and then entered, closing the door after him. He'd then run past the biometric security entrance to the vault on his left over to a wooden door directly ahead of him, unlocked it, and went through. He'd run down the hallway to another wooden door, unlocked it, went through, and then had gone down another hallway to a metal door on his left, but then stopped dead in his tracks when he heard the keys jingling on the Sam Browne belt of a member of the Armed Response Team on a random roving patrol somewhere in the book stacks of the immense Gamma Deck. And then he'd heard a voice communication between Central and Adam-13 crackle from the rover's radio, closer still. The rover was headed his way. He didn't want anyone to be able to say later that they had seen him anywhere near this area or what time they had seen him there, so Blalock had quickly tiptoe-ran to the door leading to a storage/elevator service room, opened the door, and closed it quietly behind him.

His chest rapidly rising and falling, he struggled to control his labored breathing.

What was that sound? Was the K-9 officer coming Blalock's way?

Norman's life from the day he'd met Kavitha Netram vividly flashed before his eyes…

[0000]

He'd met Kavitha on Monday, September 5th, a week to the day before he'd learned that he was not being promoted. It had also been the day that SPO James Moll had gone off the deep end...

That day had started out a typical day. He'd gone to the secure area outside the library's bank vault with Alan Katz and at 0844 hours and they had gone through the gauntlet of high-tech security measures to gain access to the bank vault door sealing off the entrance to its underground treasure trove beyond a sliding bullet-resistant door via biometric verification of authorized personnel, implemented first by Mr. Katz and then by Lt. Blalock.

First, there is the palm print scanner, followed by facial and voice recognition protocols (last name first, first name last), and the Word-of-the-Day spoken by security personnel, which is always something to do with the Bard. (The password that morning was Hamlet, if memory served). The final stage is the retinal scanner in the wall next to a gate constructed of titanium bars situated in the entrance to the alcove containing the vault door. The gate opened just as the vault door's time lock disengaged at precisely 0845. Alan twisted the dial back and forth until the four-digit combination code had been input, and then stepped aside to give Lt. Norman Blalock room to spin the vault door's big wheel and then swing the massive metal door outward...

[0000]

Lt. Blalock knocked on Chief Malcolm Leonard's open office door.

"Got a minute, Chief?"

"Sure," Chief Leonard said. "C'mon in."

Blalock stepped inside and stood before Chief

Leonard's big oak desk where he sat slowly rocking back and forth in his big, black leather chair.

"Chief, I'm concerned about Officer Moll. He's been behaving strangely the past couple of weeks...

"What do you mean?" Chief Leonard asked. "James is a good kid."

"He's behaving...irrationally," said Lt. Blalock. "One minute he seems fine and then...I don't know. He starts talking about...well, conspiracy theories. He's becoming more erratic day by day. I believe he needs to see a COPE counselor..."

"James Moll is a fine officer," Chief Leonard said matter-of-factly. "Clean-cut, neat, polite, always on time. I haven't noticed any odd behavior and I haven't gotten any complaints about him. Tell you what: just keep an eye on him for now. Anything else?"

Blalock shook his head.

Chief Leonard nodded. "Okay. That will be all. Dismissed."

Lt. Blalock turned and left the office.

Later that morning Lt. Blalock and his co-workers, SPO Peterson, who fancied himself some kind of writer, Building Services Specialist Reggie Young, and Building Services Technician Berhane Fessehaye, teased Chief Engineer Mitchell, claiming that he looked like Owiso Edera, the actor portraying Othello in the Folger's current production of the play.

SPO Peterson, a retired D.C. cop who fancied himself some kind of a writer, had kicked it off by directing Mitch's attention high above the Visitors' Entrance, Door 48, to the banner advertising the show, which featured bald Owiso/Othello holding his goateed chin and "listening" to award-winning actor Ian Merrill Peakes as Iago "whispering" into his hoop ear-ringed left ear.

"Hey, Mitch," Peterson said. "You could be Owiso's understudy for Othello."

"Go ahead, man," Mitch laughed.

Everyone looked up at the banner and then back at Mitch and immediately chided in.

"Yeah!"

"He *does* look like him!"

"He's just a little shorter."

"That's okay; he can wear platform shoes and lifts."

"Stilts!"

"Y'all need to quit, man," Mitch protested.

"Hey, Mitch, hold your chin and look serious," Peterson instigated.

Mitch complied.

They'd all laughed raucously.

Peterson kicked up the laughter by adding, "Othello Junior."

Just at that moment, the actors came out Door 48, on break from rehearsal.

Norman Blalock told them, "Hey, doesn't this guy look like Othello?"

The actors, Janie Brookshire as Desdemona, Jeff Allin as Branantio, Louis Butelli as Roderigo, Zehra Fazal as Bianca, Chris Geenbach as Montano, Joe Guzman as Lodovico, Thomas Keegan as Cassio, Todd Scofield as The Duke/Gratiano, Owiso, and Ian and his wife Karen Peakes, all stopped on the stairs and looked up at the banner and then back down to Mitch.

Norman nodded and said, "That's Mr. Othello."

Expressions of recognition animated the actors' faces. They all smiled broadly.

"Yeah!"

"He *does* look like him!"

"You can be my new understudy!"

"Othello Junior," Peterson added.

The actors laughed as they continued on their way.

Mitch smiled, shook his head, and walked away.

(From that moment on, the actors addressed Mitch as, "Mr. Othello.")

Blalock's Motorola radio on his hip crackled, "Central to Adam-3."

Lt. Blalock took his radio from his Sam Browne belt, keyed it and said, "Adam-3."

"Central to Adam-3, report to Central."

"Copy," he replied. "Responding." Blalock clipped his radio back onto his Sam Browne belt.

"Catch you guys later."

Blalock couldn't take the shortcut through the building because the Great Hall was closed for installation of the new exhibition, *Manifold Greatness: The Life and Afterlife of the King James Bible*, so he walked along the man-made plateau on the library's north façade adorned by nine larger-than-life bas-reliefs by New York sculptor John Gregory (1879–1958) depicting scenes from the Master's plays, from left to right, *A Midsommer Nights Dreame*, *Romeo and Juliet*, *The Merchant of Venice*, *Macbeth*, *Julius Caesar*, *King Lear*, *Richard III*, *Hamlet*, and *Henry IV Part I*, each beneath tall windows with Art Deco cast aluminum grilles.

He entered the building through the Research Entrance, Door 49. In the west lobby, he walked past the Gift Shop to the Guard's Desk aka Central. SPO Baylor was listening to Jazz on Pandora Internet Radio, the volume down low. The tail end of Miles Davis' *Kind of Blue* was playing.

"What's up, Fred?" Blalock asked SPO Baylor.

"Relieve me for a minute," said Fred. "I have to run downstairs."

"Sure," said Blalock.

Fred stepped from behind the desk, entered the hallway of the west wing of the building restricted to authorized personnel, turned left, and went down the stairs. Inscribed above the entrance to this section of the library is the John Milton quote:

**WHAT NEEDS MY SHAKESPEARE
FOR HIS BELOVED BONES
THE LABOR OF AN AGE
IN PILED STONES?
THOV IN OVR WONDER
AND ASTONISHMENT
HAST BVILT THYSELF
A LIVE-LONG MONVMENT**

Norman took Fred's place behind the desk just as Pandora started playing Duke Ellington's Main Title for the score of the motion picture *Anatomy of a Murder*. As if on cue, a well-dressed, raven-haired, golden-toned young beauty apparently of East Asian descent entered through Door 49. She was breathtaking, to say the least.

The stunning beauty walked directly to the guard's desk and Blalock got lost in her soul-piercing jet-black eyes. With a lyrical British accent she said, "Good morning."

"Good morning," Norman sputtered.

The exotic beauty extended her exquisite hand and Norman took it.

"I'm Kavitha Netram," she said. "I'm a new employee. I have an 11 o'clock appointment with Claire Natkin."

"I'm Norman," he said. "It's a pleasure to meet you, Ms. Netram."

"Call me Kavitha," she said.

"Call me Norman," he said. "What position?"

"I'll be working in the Gift Shop. Part-time."

"Well," Norman grinned. "We'll be seeing a lot of each other then."

Kavitha glanced over her shoulder at the Gift Shop and said, "Yes, we will."

Norman was still holding her hand. She finally looked at their clasped hands. Norman caught on and finally released her hand.

"What's that you're listening to?" Kavitha asked.

"Duke Ellington's Main Title Theme from the movie, *Anatomy of a Murder*," Norman answered.

She nodded. "Oh. Duke Ellington. DC's own."

Norman smiled. "You're familiar with his work?"

"A little," she said. "My father loves Jazz; I grew up listening to it."

"Nice," said Norman. "Well. I'll let Claire know you're here." He looked up Claire's extension in a folder on the desk, picked up the desk phone, and dialed. After a few moments, he said, "Claire, Kavitha Netram is at the front desk. Okay." He returned the receiver to its cradle and told Kavitha, "She'll be right up."

"This seems like a great place to work," she said.

"It is," said Norman.

"It isn't easy to get a job here, I can tell you that. This is my third interview."

Norman nodded.

"I'm surprised we haven't met before," she said.

"Well," Norman said, "This isn't normally my post. And I sometimes work different shifts."

"You must know an awful lot about the library," she said.

Norman nodded. "Yes, I do."

"Would you show me around sometime?"

"Certainly," Norman said. "How about tomorrow?"

Kavitha smiled. "Yes."

"Do you know what hours you'll be working?"

"One to five today," she answered, "and ten to two the rest of the week, I think."

"Can you come in a half-hour before your shift?" Norman asked.

"Yes," she said.

"It's a date," he said.

Claire Natkin entered the west lobby from the authorized personnel only section near Central, Fred Baylor right behind her.

"Hi, Kavitha," Claire said.

"Hi, Claire," said Kavitha.

"Right this way," Claire said.

"See you later," Kavitha told Norman.

Norman smiled and nodded.

Claire and Kavitha exited the lobby, Fred looking after them.

"Who is that?" SPO Baylor asked.

"Just a new employee," Norman said nonchalantly. He stepped from behind the guard's desk and said, "I'm going to check the properties. Catch you later."

Norman exited the building via Door 49, a smile on his face.

Lt. Blalock walked down the steps and turned right when he reached the sidewalk. He walked up East Capitol Street, crossed 3rd Street and proceeded to 307 East Capitol and checked the front door of the apartment building to make sure it was closed and locked. He then backtracked and went to 301 East Capitol, the Haskell Center for Education and Public Programs. Once a funeral parlor, the building houses administrative offices for the Folger Theatre, Folger Poetry, Folger Consort, and PEN/Faulkner programs, and the docents, office and meeting spaces, and hosts a variety of Folger activities, including the Folger's K-12 education programs.

Norman swiped a key fob on the electronic pad near the front door to unlock it and then opened the door and walked in past the Foulke Room, a window-filled room for seminars, meetings, and rehearsals, and walked to the elevator. He called it, got in, and took it to the third floor. He checked the building from the top down, using the stairwell to go from floor to floor, greeting everyone he encountered.

He spoke to Education Programs Assistant Caitlin Griffin, Public Programs Assistant Elaine Johnson, Elementary School Programs Coordinator Lucretia Anderson, Assistant Artistic Producer Beth Emelson, Head of External Relations Garland Scott, and Education Outreach Coordinator Danielle Drakes.

When he reached the first floor, he exited the building through the back door and stepped onto its private parking lot. He walked off the parking lot, turned left on 3rd Street, SE and walked up the stairs of apartment building 10, checked the front door, then walked back to the sidewalk. He checked the front doors of apartment buildings 16, 18, and 22 and found that they were all locked.

Lt. Blalock took his Motorola radio from his belt, keyed it, and spoke into it. "Adam-3 to Central."

"Central. Go ahead, sir."

"Activity normal in 301, which is secure, front and rear. All outside properties secure at this time."

"10-4, Adam-3, at 11:07 hours."

Blalock clipped his radio back onto his belt and crossed the street past the Capitol Police guard booth in front of a parking lot located between the John Adams building of the Library of Congress and the rear of the Folger Shakespeare Library.

He checked the Folger's garden gate grill, outside Double-Door 34, and Door 21, and then notified Central that they were all secure.

"Copy, Adam-3, at 11:08 hours," SPO Baylor acknowledged over the radio.

Blalock continued on, turned the corner and walked through Puck Circle, the Folger's private parking lot on the west side of the building, past the cast aluminum balcony balustrade on the balcony, which features Shakespeare's coat of arms – complete with motto, "Non Sans Droict": "Not Without Right" – repeated six times along its length, and the aluminum replica of the Puck sculpture by Brenda Putnam, on display behind a water fountain, facing Congress.

Inscribed beneath the statue, like the restored original now housed in the Elizabethan Theatre lobby to protect it from the ravages of acid rain and vandals, is the line from *A Midsommer Night's Dreame*, "What fooles these mortals be!"

He turned right at the corner of the building and walked up the stairs to Door 49, the Research Entrance, just as Special Events Manager Rebecca Scott was exiting. He held the door open for her.

"Good morning, Norm," she smiled.

"Good morning, Rebecca. How are you today?"

"Hanging in there. How about you?"

"Fine, thank you," he said. "I'll see you later."

"See you."

Before Blalock could get through the door, he saw something that made him stop in his tracks: SPO James Moll.

Sometime between check off from work the previous day and check in the following morning, SPO James Moll, Jr., had decided to make a bold fashion statement.

SPO Moll reported for duty dressed as usual in a cleaned and pressed Folger Library Special Police Officer's uniform, work shoes shining, sporting a funky-fresh haircut, the front and around the sides of his head nicely trimmed and shaped up…but halfway down the back of his head cornrows picked up. Cornrows. Long cornrows that ran down to the middle of his back. With tiny seashells on the tips of each and every one of them, Stevie Wonder style. Colorful shells.

"What's up, lieutenant?" he said as he breezed past Norman and went into the building.

Lt. Blalock followed him in. Mouths agape, SPOs Fred Baylor and Helen Rowe, along with Kavitha and other staffers and patrons, stared at James Moll.

SPO Moll's movements were exaggerated as he moved his head to turn his gaze to speak to this coworker and that visitor, as though he liked to work his cornrows, the seashells clacking together as the cornrows running down his back swished from one shoulder to the other. He seemed to be showing them off, as though they were his own. Well, they were actually. He had the receipt to prove it.

He hadn't had time to grow them, so they were obviously extensions woven to the short hair on the back of his head. Unbelievable.

"J. Moll," he kept saying. "J. Moll, y'all."

Lt. Blalock took James Moll by the arm. "Come on, let's talk, officer."

Norman took James Moll into the authorized personnel only section and down the stairs to the Security Office. He closed the door.

"What the hell is wrong with you?" Blalock asked.

"What?" James Moll said. "I have the right to express myself."

"Do you have a drug problem?" Blalock wanted to know.

"Hell naw," Officer Moll told him.

"You're a special police officer," said Blalock. "You can't work here or anywhere as an SPO looking like that. You know this, man. Take the day off, take that shit out of your hair, and come back here tomorrow compliant with our appearance code and all will be forgiven. Otherwise, we've got to let you go."

"Well, I quit!" James yelled. He snatched his badge from his shirt and threw it across the room. "I'm tired of this place anyway. This ain't nothing but a church to an idol! I don't worship Shakespeare; Jesus Christ is my Lord and Savior! I'm out of here!"

James Moll stormed from the office and slammed the door behind him.

Lt. Blalock shook his head. He took his radio from his Sam Browne belt and called Central as he followed James Moll out of the office.

"Adam-3 to Central, James Moll no longer works here. He's on his way up; make sure he leaves the building."

"Central copy," SPO Baylor acknowledged.

"I'm on my way up," Lt. Blalock advised. "Adam-3 to Adam-1."

"Adam-1."

"Please meet me at Central, sir."

"Adam-1 copy. Responding."

On the way up the steps, Lt. Blalock could hear James Moll yelling in the west lobby. When he got there, SPO Baylor and SPO Rowe had James by the arms, dragging him toward Door 49.

Awestruck patrons and staffers, including Special Events Manager Rebecca Scott, Controller Howard Parks, Cataloger Amelia Davis, Rare Bindings Specialist Frank Mowery, Building Services Coordinator Dot Morgan, Executive Assistant Karen Lyon, Staff Associate Ruth Hollinger, Head of Collection Information Services Jim Kuhn, Librarian Stephen Ennis, and Director Mike Witmore, were watching the spectacle.

Chief Leonard made his way through the crowd of staffers standing in the hallway and entered the west lobby right behind Lt. Blalock.

"Come on, James," Baylor said. "You've got to go."

"What are y'all looking at?" James screamed. "Ain't nothing wrong with me, it's all y'all that's fucked up! Worshipping Shakespeare, worshipping the Folgers! They ain't gods! They ain't gods! Thou shalt not worship idols before me!

"You're all puppets of the three city states: the City of London, Vatican City and Washington, DC, which are not part of the nations they control. These sovereign, corporate entities have their own laws, their own identities, and their own flags. We're all subordinate to the Crown! We are not free! We are not free! Wake up! Wake up!"

With the help of Chief Leonard and Lt. Blalock, James Moll's coworkers finally got him outside.

"Don't come back here," Chief Leonard told James.

"You're banned from the building. Show your face here again and you'll be arrested on the spot."

"Fuck you!" James yelled. "I ain't *never* comin' back here! This is Satan's lair. Y'all do the devil's work. The devil's work! The truth is the mortal enemy of the lie!"

James Moll stormed to the parking lot, climbed into his 2001 Toyota Corolla, slammed the door, and burned rubber backing out of the parking lot onto 2nd Street, SE, and peeled off down the street. A United States Capitol Police officer who witnessed James' reckless driving turned on the light bar of his police car and gave chase.

"What the hell was that all about?" asked Chief Leonard. "What was up with his hair?"

"Let's go to your office, chief," said Lt. Blalock. "I'll fill you in."

"Okay," Chief Leonard agreed. "Fred, get started on the paperwork to ban James from the building. I'll hook up with you later."

"Yes, sir," said SPO Baylor.

Lt. Blalock and Chief Leonard went back into the building. SPOs Rowe and Baylor lingered out front for awhile, shaking their heads and looking in the direction James had sped away.

O brave new world, that has such people in't.

Back inside, Chief Leonard reassured the startled and dismayed crowd.

"Sorry for the disturbance," he cajoled. "That individual obviously has personal problems and has become emotionally disturbed, but I want to assure you that at no time were any of you in danger. There is nothing for you to worry about. That poor man just needs help and we're going to see that he gets it. Please, patrons, enjoy the rest of your visit, and staff, go on about your business as usual. Everyone is safe."

Everyone thought what he said was reasonable so the

crowd began to disperse.

Lt. Blalock followed Chief Leonard back to his office. On the way down the hall, Chief Leonard whispered to Blalock, "Order a watch for that nut. He could do anything. He could vandalize the exterior of the building, red spray-paint graffiti on the walls…or the statue of Puck. You can imagine. 'My name is Puck and I love to…'"

"Or he could come back with a gun," Lt. Blalock offered.

Chief Leonard stepped into his office, slammed the door, and continued, "If that maniac vandalizes the place, whoever is on watch will be out there standing in the unemployment line right next to that crazy sonofabitch! Spread the word."

Lt. Blalock nodded and said, "Yes, sir."

[0000]

On the night of September 5th, strains of Benny Goodman wafting over them, Norman had a candlelight dinner at his place with his squeeze Leah Rosa Hinton, a copper-toned Ameri-Rican honey with a law degree and dancer's legs. They discussed over pasta the incident involving James Moll, as his Black Labrador/Great Dane Mix Bruno sat nearby, watching every bite they took, ever vigilant for a tasty morsel from his master's table.

"Well," Leah asked, "What do you think drove him over the edge?"

Norman shrugged.

"You sure it wasn't your workplace that pushed him over the edge?"

"Who knows," Norman said. "He's a conspiracy nut, the man's paranoid."

"Just because you think everybody is out to get you," Leah argued, "doesn't mean it isn't true."

Norman considered Leah's argument and then shook his head.

"Everybody I've met at your job is a little off, you included."

"What do you mean?" Norman asked.

"Don't get offended," she said, "but it's true. All of you are slightly…off. You, for instance. Not only do you work at a museum, surrounded by billions of dollars worth of shit that nobody wants to steal, but you spend most of your spare time visiting museums, *and* you *live* in a museum. And all you wear is your dead daddy's old ass clothes…"

My wardrobe is *vintage*," Norman corrected her.

"Old ass clothes," Leah corrected him. "And those Bogart hats…

"Fedoras, Leah."

"Whatever, Norm. You dress like an old B&W movie detective! And you're always listening to old ass music and watching old ass B&W movies…and the History

25

Channel…or got your face buried in a history book. And you know everything there is to know about Shakespeare…"

"*Nobody* knows everything about Shakespeare," Norman corrected her.

"The point is, Norman, that the past is more important to you than the present. And the future too, seems like."

"Now, wait a minute," Norman protested. "You've twisted this all around and turned this into the marriage argument? Really? No, you didn't."

"I'm getting old," she said. "I'll be 35 next month. I want to have kids."

"You've got to hook up with someone who can do that, baby. I can't. I told you, I am not making my own grandkids. It's me time and I don't have much time left. I can't spend it changing diapers…and neither can you.

"Imagine, you smell doody and you chase junior down only to find he's clean. And then he looks up at you with his big brown eyes and says, 'I no do-do. Dada. Dada do-do.'

They laughed for awhile before Leah got serious again.

"Let's face it, Norm, the only thing we have going for us is great sex. And you owe your performance to Cialis for daily use."

Norman shrugged. "Better living through chemistry. A man's got to do what a man's got to do."

"I've found somebody," she said flatly.

"That's good," he said.

"I'm leaving you, Norman."

"I know, Leah. I've known that from the day we hooked up three years ago."

They ate the rest of their dinner in silence.

[0000]

The next morning, Tuesday, September 6th, Norman gave Kavitha a tour.

He informed her that the private research library, which was designed by notable Philadelphia architect Paul Philippe Cret, was dedicated on April 23, 1932 and is listed in the National Register of Historic Places, is accessible only to doctorate and post doctorate scholars who have been approved by the Amherst Board of Trustees to receive Readers Cards, with the exceptions of the Gift Shop, the Great Hall, the Shakespeare Gallery, the Elizabethan Theatre, the Anne Hathaway Gallery, and the Elizabethan Garden, which are open to the general public. However, certain restricted areas are open to the public once a year, on or about April 23rd, the Bard's birthday.

On the library's neoclassical exterior, he pointed out on the west and east ends of its north façade the two glass and Art Deco cast aluminum double front doors that match the grilles over the tall windows above the nine bas-reliefs of scenes from Shakespeare's plays by the New York sculptor John Gregory, artwork which by convention would ordinarily have been positioned much higher, near the top of the building, however, the Folgers asked for the placement near street level to give the public a better view. He directed her attention to the winged horse Pegasus carved on the planters on either side of the staircases to these doors; the masks of Comedy and Tragedy displayed above these doors, Tragedy on the east side, Comedy on the west.

On the inside of the library, Norman explained that the design evokes Tudor England with elements such as oak paneling, ornamental floor tile, and high plaster ceilings.

"I can't show you the Great Hall right now," he told her, "because it's closed for installation of the new exhibition. Right now, I can show you the Old and New Readings Rooms, the Founders' Room, and the Elizabethan Theatre."

"Sounds great," Kavitha said. "Say, what was up with that guard yesterday?"

"He's a conspiracy theory fanatic," Norman explained. "All those conspiracy theories knocking around in his head must have finally driven him over the edge."

"What did he mean by three city states," she wanted to know.

Supposedly," Norman said, "the three city states are interconnected and control the world. Allegedly, the City of London's powerbase is finance, Washington, DC's powerbase is the military, and Vatican City's powerbase is the Catholic religion."

"I see," she said.

"Back to the library. In 1879, Henry Folger's interest in Shakespeare was sparked by a lecture given by Ralph Waldo Emerson that he attended as a senior at Amherst College. Throughout a long career in the oil industry, Henry, with his wife's assistance, acquired the world's largest collection of Shakespeare materials. Together, Henry and his wife Emily planned this library to house their immense collection, which was stored in warehouses in New York and New Jersey. Henry died before the library was built, but Emily realized his dream. *Their* dream."

"It's a love story," Kavitha said. "A story of love that reaches from beyond the grave."

"That's very poetic," Norman said. "Yes, I suppose you're right. Emily's love for Henry kept their dream alive after he was dead. This place is their legacy. They didn't have children, but together they created this library."

"You're wrong," said Kavitha. "This library *is* their baby."

"Hmmm," Norman said. "I never thought about it that way. Come on; let's start in the Gail Paster Reading Room, formerly known as the Old Reading Room. This way."

Kavitha followed Norman into the restricted area off the west lobby to a door on the left. He opened it for her and then followed her inside.

"Hi, Eric," Blalock said. "This is a new employee, Kavitha. I'm just taking her in for a look."

"Hi," Eric said. He shook Kavitha's hand. "Enjoy."

Kavitha followed Norman to double wood and glass doors and into the Gail Paster Reading Room. Norman put a finger to his lips and then whispered, "We don't want to disturb the readers. Come on." He directed her attention to the Seven Ages of Man stained glass window on the west wall above the entrance they had just walked through.

"The Seven Ages of Man window is by the Philadelphia stained-glass studio of Nicola d'Ascenzo, depicting the Seven Ages of Man that Jaques describes in *As You Like It*. Most of the 'ages' that Jaques describes are self-explanatory. The sixth one, the pantaloon, comes from the Italian comedy character Pantalone, and refers to a feeble old man. At Henry Folger's request, D'Ascenzo modeled the stone tracery of the window after the apse window of Stratford's Holy Trinity Church.

"D'Ascenzo also did windows at the Yale and Princeton university chapels, the memorial chapel at Valley Forge, and the Washington National Cathedral."

"It's beautiful," Kavitha whispered.

"Come this way," he said.

She followed him.

"This is the New Reading Room," Norman told her. "It was designed by Warren Cox of Hartman-Cox Architects and was constructed in the early 1980s as a modern complement to the Old Reading Room. These wooden pillars leading from the old room into the new room and high, stone-trimmed arches are a tribute to Paul Cret's original design.

"The glass panes overhead let in indirect daylight, making it an excellent workspace for scholars. The paintings on the walls are from the Folger's own collection."

"It's magnificent," Kavitha said.

Norman nodded. "Come on."

Kavitha followed him back into the Gail Paster Reading Room. He stopped.

"I'll take you through here again sometime when no one is here," Blalock whispered. "But while we're here, direct your attention to the back wall." He pointed. "In that alcove there, between the portraits of Emily and Henry, see that memorial plaque?"

Kavitha nodded.

"Behind that memorial plaque is a columbarium niche containing the urns of Mr. and Mrs. Folger."

"You're joking," Kavitha gasped.

"No," Norman assured her. "Come on, let's go."

Norman led Kavitha out the way they came and then turned left.

Speaking in a normal voice, he pointed out the Director's Office on the right and the Librarian's Office on the left on the way to the Founders' Room at the end of the hall. On the right, just outside the entrance to the Founders' Room, was a counter with storage underneath where Monday – Friday, Event Services Assistant Madeleine Torres set up urns of regular and decaf coffee and hot water, and tea bags and a pitcher of ice cold water, along with white paper cups, coffee creamer, and sugar and artificial sweetener for consumption by staff and readers, although food and drink are prohibited in the Gail Paster and New Reading Rooms, for obvious reasons. Madeleine kept the love coming all day long, making sure the tea and coffee kept flowing, up until about 2:30 when she cleared it away and set up for Tea Time in the Tea Room in the basement, located near to the restaurant grade kitchen, across the hall from the offices of IT and HR.

A well-groomed young man walked up to the counter and poured himself a cup of coffee.

"Mike," Norman said, "have you met our new gift shop employee, Kavitha?"

"No," said Mike. He shook Kavitha's hand. "Nice to meet you."

"Kavitha, this is Mike Witmore."

"Nice to meet you," Kavitha said. "Norman...Lt. Blalock is just showing me around."

"You're in good hands," said Mike. "Nobody knows this place better than Norman. Enjoy. See you around."

Mike turned and walked down the hall back to his office.

"You call the director by his first name?" Kavitha whispered.

"We're on a first name basis around here," Norman told her. "All of us. Come on."

They went into the Founders' Room.

"The Founders' Room," Norman said, "was originally designed as a private space for Henry and Emily Folger. Now it's a meeting room and a lounge for 'readers.' And off to the left there is Chief Leonard's office.

"Note how the opaque leaded-glass windows, carved paneling and beams, antique furniture, and the stone fireplace create a Tudor atmosphere. The figures in the windows represent Shakespearean characters, among them Julius Caesar, Henry V, Hamlet, Cleopatra, and Ophelia.

"The curio cabinets hold changing displays of materials related to the Folgers and their collection. On display right now are Shakespeare characters rendered in metal, various porcelain figures, a Wedgwood chess piece of notable 19th Century actress Sarah Siddons as Lady Macbeth, photos of the founders, and Henry Clay Folger's ticket to Ralph Waldo Emerson's 1879 lecture at Amherst College. This lecture inspired Henry Folger to become a scholar of Shakespeare and an avid collector of First Folios and Shakespeareana..."

Kavitha interrupted, "Having worked here for so long, do you still marvel at the influence of Shakespeare?"

"Every day," Norman said matter-of-factly. "He did

well for himself, even in life, which is quite an achievement considering the times he lived in. In spite of it all, he was a wealthy man, unlike most artists who end up penniless but earn others millions, even in our times. But in his day, the theater's chief competition for an audience was public executions and bear-bating..."

"What's that?" Kavitha interrupted.

"Well," said Norman, "Bear-baiting was a popular bloodsport in England. Arenas called bear-gardens, which consisted of circular fenced areas known as 'pits', with raised seating for the eager spectators, were packed with bloodthirsty fans. Each of these bear-gardens had at the edge of the pit a post set in the ground where they chained the bear, either by the neck or the leg. And then they'd set a number of well-trained hunting dogs on it, replacing them as they became exhausted or got maimed or killed by the bear. Sometimes they'd turn the bear loose so it could chase after animals or people. For a long time, the main bear-garden in London was the Paris Garden.

"Henry VIII was a fan and had a pit constructed at Whitehall. Elizabeth I was also fond of the entertainment."

"Why, that's dreadful!" Kavitha gasped.

Norman shrugged. "That's entertainment."

Kavitha shuddered.

"Where was I?" said Norman. "Yes. In the back there in those locked, glass enclosed bookcases is the London Collection, which was donated by Ambassador and Mrs. George C. McGhee. The book cases' 22 shelves contain about 16 books per shelf. The books in this valuable collection include *The Great Fire of London* by Walter C. Bell, *The Private Palaces of London* by E. Beresford Chancellor, and *The Man of Pleasure* by Ralph Neville.

"There are a few important paintings in here as well. The 'Sieve' portrait of Queen Elizabeth I, the Virgin Queen, circa 1579, painted by George Gower, and Catherine Trentham, Lady Stanhope, circa 1615, painted by William

Larkin, a London-based portrait artist famous for producing high-quality portraits like this, and the Ashbourne Portrait of Sir Hugh Hamersley, Lord Mayor of London in 1627, artist unknown."

Kavitha said, "I heard that this is really a portrait of Edward de Vere, the 17th Earl of Oxford. I heard the Folgers purchased it thinking it was a portrait of Shakespeare. I seem to remember something about the Folgers being accused of altering the painting in the late 20s or early 30s to make it look more like Shakespeare?"

"Well," said Blalock, "The original alterations to the Hamersley painting, to make it look like a Shakespeare portrait, are believed to be the handiwork of painter Clement Kingston. In 1979, the Folger commissioned Peter Michaels to restore the portrait. He uncovered the coat of arms, and his assistant Lisa Oehrl made a sketch of it, unaware of the sitter's identity. It was Lilly Lievsay, Folger cataloguer of manuscripts, and Folger curator Laetitia Yeandle who linked the image of the sketch conclusively to the family crest of Hugh Hamersley. The restoration clarified the date of the portrait as well. The date had been changed from 1612 to 1611, the year Shakespeare was 47. In 1612, Hugh Hamersley was 47, though he had not been granted a coat of arms at that time. It is the conjecture of Art Historian William Pressly that they were either painted on later or included in anticipation of the honor.

"Though they were disappointed, some Oxfordians accepted the results, and claimed partial credit for the discovery. However, the identity of the sitter is still believed to be de Vere by some Oxfordians, despite the fact that Edward de Vere died in 1604, eight years before the portrait was painted."

"You really know your stuff," Kavitha complimented him.

Norman shrugged. "If you work around here long enough, you pick up things."

Kavitha looked around the Founders' Room and beamed, "This is all so fascinating!"

"Yes," Norman agreed. "We even rent spaces here for special events like parties, weddings, inaugural balls, even a memorial service once." He rubbed his fingers together at her eye level. "For big bucks. Come on, I'll show you the Elizabethan Theatre."

Kavitha followed Norman out of the Founders' Room, back down the hall, and down the staircase on their right to the basement. When they exited the stairwell, they made two right turns and proceeded down a tunnel, past the Mail Room, the Security Office, and the offices of Photography and Digital Imaging. Photos of artwork, costumes, singers, actors, and politicians such as President Bill Clinton and Senator John Kerry adorned the tunnel walls.

"Why did the Folgers pick this site for the library?" Kavitha asked.

"They chose this site during World War I, when they walked from Union Station to Capitol Hill and strolled around the neighborhood while their travel was delayed. Emily was familiar with this area and she liked it. Derelict rowhouses were here at that time and the United States Supreme Court hadn't yet been built, nor had the John Adams building of the Library of Congress. The cornerstone for the Supreme Court building was laid in October of 1932 and was completed in 1935. The John Adams building opened in December of 1938. The cornerstone of the Folger was laid in June of 1930 and it was dedicated on April 23, 1932, on Shakespeare's birthday."

They walked past the women guards' locker room on the left, boxes of supplies on their right, and then on their right the door to the Facilities Office and a stairwell going down to a hallway that ultimately leads to the dressing rooms and the backstage of the Elizabethan Theatre.

Norman opened Door 12 and held it open for her.

They stepped into a storage area with a metal door on the left and a wooden door directly in front of them. They went through the wooden door and stepped into the Anne Hathaway Gallery. Public restrooms were directly ahead of them, a small display case containing literature regarding Othello was on their left, a large display case containing stage swords and information regarding stage combat on their right.

They proceeded right and walked up a two-flight staircase covered in slate and then past the Docents' Desk.

An attractive woman with a short haircut exited the box office.

"Hey, Caroline," Norman said.

"Hey, Norm," she replied.

"Have you met our new gift shop employee, Kavitha?"

"No." Caroline walked over and shook Kavitha's hand.

"This is Caroline Bedinger. She's in charge of special events. Caroline brings in the big bucks. If it wasn't for her, the place would go out of business."

Caroline sucked her teeth and threw a hand at Blalock. "Yeah, okay, Norm. It was nice meeting you, Kavitha."

"Nice meeting you," said Kavitha,

"See you around," said Caroline as she headed into the Great Hall.

"Before we go into the theatre," Norman said, "let me introduce you to Puck. This is the original statue created for the Folger grounds by the award-winning sculptor Brenda Putnam in 1932 and restored in 2001. It was originally outside in Puck Circle, located at the west end of the building. Ravaged by the elements and vandals, it was brought inside for safekeeping. An aluminum replica is now in Puck Circle."

Norman opened one of the Elizabethan Theatre's

double-doors and held it open for Kavitha. She stepped inside and he followed her in.

"In Shakespeare's day, inns sometimes served as playhouses, so to evoke the courtyard of an English Renaissance inn, this intimate theatre, which has a seating capacity of only 253, has three-tiered wooden balconies, carved oak columns, and half-timbered façade. Overhead, the canopy represents the sky.

"See what's inscribed on the canopy?"

Kavitha looked up and read aloud, "All the world's a stage and all the men and women merely players."

"Ain't that the truth," Blalock said.

Kavitha nodded and said, "Here at the Folger, your uniform is your costume. You're not a security guard..."

"I just play one in real life," Norman finished her sentence.

They laughed.

"Come on" he said, "I'll show you the Elizabethan Garden."

Kavitha followed Norman out of the theatre to Door 48 and through a set of wood and glass double-doors. Norman removed a large ring of keys from his belt, unlocked one of the glass and aluminum outer doors, and they stepped outside. Kavitha followed him down the stairs.

"The garden's right over here," Norman said. "I go there all the time. It's a nice place to collect your thoughts."

"You're very knowledgeable, Norman." Kavitha said.

Norman shrugged. "Everything I've told you is on the Folger website."

"Not the information about the three city states," she countered.

"No, but it's all over the Internet," he said.

"You're just being modest," she argued.

"I'm just a building guard," he said. "What do I know?"

"No," she said. "You're a teacher."

Norman did not comment.

"How long have you been working here?" she wanted to know.

"Twenty-five years," he told her.

"I guess no one knows this building better than you, huh?"

"Nobody alive anyway," he said.

Kavitha smiled and nodded.

He let her walk through the garden gate first and then followed her into the garden.

"Welcome to the Elizabethan Garden," Norm said. "It features a knot garden inspired by herbal references in Shakespeare's plays..."

[0000]

On the morning of September 12th, the ever dapper Chief Malcolm Leonard, wearing one of his many tailor made suits, called Blalock into his office and gave him the bad news.

Slowly rocking back and forth in his big, black leather chair, Chief Leonard said, "I'm sorry, Norm, but the committee decided to hire from the outside for the captain position. The deciding factor was that you don't have a bachelor's degree.

"Say, do you remember that old CLEP commercial featuring Abraham Lincoln, where a job placement counselor asks Honest Abe about his qualifications? Abe says, 'I've done a lot of reading and studying, sort of on my own.' And the cigar-chomping counselor says, 'You ain't goin' nowhere without that sheepskin, fella.'

"Well, it's the same thing here. But you're going to like the new guy. Name's Nathan Rockford. He's retired MPD. Great guy. I'll introduce you to him later today.

"While I've got you, Norm, there's something else I've been meaning to talk to you about. I think it's time you seriously started thinking about retirement. It's time we bring in more new blood.

"You know, just a few short years ago, you would have never let that James Moll incident occur. Face it, buddy, you're past it..."

"Surely, you're not blaming me for that fiasco, Chief. I warned you about him, I told you he needed help..."

"Norm," Chief Leonard interrupted, "your job is to make me look good. You didn't do that. Bottom line." He looked at his watch. "Damn, I'm late for a meeting. Got to run."

The Chief of Safety and Security got up from his big, black leather chair behind his big oak desk and left his office, leaving Norman sitting there.

Oh, how Norman longed for the good old days when

the legendary Lenny Mason was the Chief of Safety and Security.

[0000]

Later on the morning of September 12th, Lt. Blalock stood in the Elizabethan Garden, studying the Wyatt sculpture of Julius Caesar as he considered his dismal future. He was pulled away from his thoughts when the Motorola radio on his hip crackled with a female's voice, "Central to Adam-3."

SPO Blalock took his radio from his belt, keyed it and said, "Adam-3."

"Central to Adam-3, report to Central."

"Copy," he replied. "Responding."

Blalock returned the radio to his Sam Browne belt and then strode away from the Julius Caesar sculpture, through the open gateway, up the east steps flanked by two marble benches and through one of the double aluminum doors at Door 48, the theater entrance of the building, a mask of Comedy rising from the stone above the entry. He proceeded through the second set of double doors made of Oak and into the into the Elizabethan Theatre lobby, an Elizabethan style chandelier with electric "candles" overhead, double doors of the theater itself flanked by the original Brenda Putnam Alabama marble statue of Puck and the wooden Docent's Desk directly ahead, the Box Office and stairwell to the theater balcony to his left, and on his right the Great Hall. Standing post there at the entrance to the theater lobby was SPO Peterson.

"How's it going, Q?" asked Lt. Blalock.

"Good, Norm," SPO Peterson replied. "You?"

"Good," Lt. Blalock lied. "Catch you later." He waved at the Docent on duty. "Hi, Gina."

Gina Guglielmo waved and replied, "Good morrow, Norman!"

Blalock nodded. "I'll talk with you later."

Norman Blalock proceeded through the Great Hall with its 30-foot-high plaster strapwork ceiling adorned here and there with Shakespeare's coat of arms, Appalachian white oak paneling, and ornamental floor tiles, where the current exhibition, *Manifold Greatness: The Life and Afterlife of the King James Bible,* was now open to the public.

Waiting for him in the west lobby at the Guard's Desk aka Central, where SPO LaTanya Gant was currently assigned, he found Chief Leonard, and a tall and muscular man with close cut hair and military bearing, who was crammed into a snug-fitting, off the rack blue suit.

Blalock looked over at Kavitha Netram, who was a scant few feet away from Central. Today she was wearing something blue, a short dress, he hoped. He'd check her out later when she was up and around helping customers, or bending over to get supplies or something out of a low drawer.

"Hey, Tanya," Blalock greeted Gant, who nodded at him. "Chief."

"Norm," Chief Leonard said, "I'd like you to meet Nathan Rockford, our new captain."

Captain Rockford thrust out a massive paw and Norman Blalock took it.

"Nice to meet you," Rockford said.

Lt. Blalock pried his hand from the captain's bear-grip and nodded. "Captain."

"Call me Rocky," Captain Rockford grinned.

"You know Kavitha?" asked the chief. "She started working here at the gift shop last week."

Lt. Blalock didn't bother to mention that he had a rapport with the extremely bright, gorgeous and shapely young beauty. Instead, he simply said, "How are you,

Kavitha?"

Kavitha smiled and answered, "Fine. How about you?"

"Good," Norman Blalock lied.

"Norm," said the chief, "please make arrangements to show them around, an overview for Kavitha and a grand tour for Rocky. I'd do it, but I have to attend Safety and Security Committee meetings all week."

Blalock didn't bother to mention that he'd already given Kavitha a private tour, he simply said, "Sure thing."

"I can't do it today," said Rocky. "Stack of paperwork to fill out in HR."

"How about tomorrow morning?" Blalock wanted to know. "Is that good for both of you?"

"Yes," they said.

Blalock nodded

"Good," Chief Leonard said. "Catch you later. C'mon, Rocky."

The chief and his Ex-O turned and walked down the hall.

Tanya waited until she was certain that the chief and the ex-o were out of earshot and then said, "I just want you to know that I'm sorry you didn't get the job. You're made for it. Hell, you should have been promoted to chief five years ago."

Norman shrugged. "Management just decided to go another way, that's all."

"Well," Tanya offered, "If you had a bachelor's degree and they'd turned you down, you'd have a good lawsuit."

Blalock changed the subject. "Say, Tanya, are you going to the Hawk 'n' Dove tonight? You know it's going out of business. Some of us are getting together over there tonight, you know, saying goodbye to the place."

Tanya shrugged. "I might stop by."

"Later," Norman said.

Kavitha stood and caught Norman's attention. Norman Blalock stopped in his tracks and watched her lift the desk-door and walk out from the cash register stand. Face and limbs the color of polished brass, she was dressed in a short teal mist blue dress, her firm, smooth, shapely legs accented by sensible heals. She sauntered over to a display/storage area directly in front of Central, and bent over to unlock the double doors beneath the display table. She took her sweet time finding what she was looking for and then sauntered back into the Gift Shop.

Norm sighed. And then noticed Tanya looking at him.

"Got to go," he said.

Lt. Norman Blalock ran up the three steps leading into an authorized personnel only zone of the Folger.

That night, right after the people Norman came with left, Kavitha Netram, dressed in a form-fitting little black dress, sat down at his table in a corner of one of the crowded rooms at the *Hawk 'n' Dove* restaurant on Capitol Hill, which was going out of business after 44 years. She set a glass of what he was having in front of him.

While she looked him over Kavitha sipped through a cocktail straw what appeared to be an Appletini.

They had to speak up to be heard above the music and the din of the crowd.

"Hello, Kavitha."

"Hello, Norman."

"I'm surprised to see you here," he said.

"A pleasant surprise, I hope," she said.

Norman nodded. "Certainly."

He held up the glass of cognac she'd set in front of him and said, "Thanks."

"My pleasure," Kavitha said. "I just wanted to repay you for the tour of the Folger last week. You taught me a lot about the place. For instance, I never knew that urns containing the Folgers' ashes are entombed in a columbarium niche behind that plaque in the back wall of the Gail Paster Reading Room. Their library is actually their tomb. Incredible." She raised her glass. "Thank you."

Blalock raised his glass of Hennessy. "You're welcome." He sipped his drink and then set it down.

Norman fell silent. He couldn't figure out why the hell a young looker like Kavitha was sitting there talking to an old-timer. The fact of the matter was that he was blown away and rendered speechless. Never before had an object of his desire presented itself so miraculously. He didn't believe in miracles.

After a few moments, she said, "Norm, today I overheard you and Tanya Gant discussing how you were passed over for promotion..."

"Really," Norm said flatly.

"It's a shame," Kavitha said. "I agree with Tanya. Nobody is more qualified for the position than you, I'm sure. It's a travesty really. I'm sorry."

Norm shrugged. "The hiring committee just decided to go another way." After a moment he asked, "How did you know I was here?"

"I overheard you telling Officer Gant that you'd be here tonight to say farewell to this place."

"I see," Norm said. "You overhear a lot."

Kavitha laughed. "The guard's desk is only a couple of feet from the gift shop. I can't help but overhear the guard's talking, even when they're whispering."

Norm nodded and said, "Yeah."

Kavitha sipped her drink and then said, "I also overheard Officer Gant say you were passed over because you don't have a bachelor's degree. I find it hard to believe that you even need a degree for that position after being on the job for decades. You're the best man for the job. Period. You remind me of my history professor." She sighed and rolled her eyes. "I had a terrible crush on him."

"Really?" Norm said.

"Of course, Norm. He was knowledgeable…and attractive. Very sexy. Just like you."

Norman rolled his eyes and shook his head.

"I've just been listening to Folger docents for 25 years," he countered. "I'm just repeating what I've heard…"

"No, Norman, it's more than that."

"If you say so," he said. "Really, I'm just a good listener and I remember what I read, that's all." He quickly changed the subject. "So what's your degree in?"

"I have a doctorate in art history," she answered, "from Oxford University."

"Then why are you working in the Folger Gift Shop, doctor?"

Kavitha shrugged. "It's just something to earn a little money while I track down the job I'm looking for, something in my field."

Blalock nodded.

Kavitha picked up a folded black tee shirt off the table. "I see you got your souvenir tee shirt. *Hawk 'n' Dove, Last Call.* It's a nice memento."

Norman took the tee shirt from her and put it back on the table. He looked at her for a time and then asked, "What is this, Kavitha?"

"C'mon. I've enjoyed our conversations at work, but why are you buttering up an old Billy goat like me? What's *really* going on? What do you want?"

She smiled. "You're very perceptive. Most men don't question, they just follow their dream and go with the flow…"

"The dream of sleeping with you?" Norm asked. "Listen, if it's a Sugar Daddy you're looking for, you've got the wrong man. I'm a Splenda Daddy: sweet, but not the real thing."

Kavitha laughed. It was delightful and infectious. Norm could not help but laugh along with her.

When she caught her breath, she leaned in and said,

"My employer will make you a rich man if you acquire something for him from the Folger's vault, something that will never be missed."

She sipped her fruity cocktail and looked him in the eye.

Norman raised an eyebrow. He gulped his cognac and then stared at her.

"The Folger has impeccable security, Dr. Netram. It can't be done."

"Kavitha, Norm, call me Kavitha, just like always. We're friends."

"Yeah, right," Norman snapped. "Become a thief for me, Norm, go to prison for me. We're friends, Norm. Ha!"

"My employer needs an inside man. He needs *you*, Norman. We can pull off this job. You won't get caught and you will be well paid."

He glared at her.

"Something extremely valuable that won't be missed?" Norm pondered.

Kavitha Netram nodded.

Norman looked her in the eye and said, "Stolen valuables will *always* be missed, Kavitha...especially at the Folger."

Kavitha smirked.

"Not if no one knows the valuable item was ever there," she said.

He tilted his head.

Kavitha smiled and then got deadly serious. "I'll arrange a meeting with him. You should at least hear him out before you turn him down. What have you got to lose?"

[0000]

On the night of September 13th, Kavitha arranged for a limousine to pick him up at 8:00 alongside of Lincoln Park on Capitol Hill, near where he lived in a Victorian rowhouse built circa 1926. Kavitha, wearing a form-fitting short gray dress with black silk stockings and three-inch gray pumps and smelling, as always, of expensive shampoo, body wash, lotion, and perfume, was waiting for him inside the black Lincoln limo, listening to Duke Ellington. She was smirking and holding a Martini in each of her exquisite, manicured hands. When he'd gotten comfortable in his seat, she handed him one of them.

"Nice suit," she said. "Nice hat."

"Thanks," he said. "Nice dress."

"Thank you."

"Duke Ellington and His Orchestra performing *Things Ain't What They Used to Be*," Blalock observed. "From the soundtrack of Cabin in the Sky. You pick this music?"

Kavitha nodded.

"I'm impressed," said Norman.

Kavitha smiled. Norman raised his drink and Kavitha tapped her Martini glass against his.

They were driven to an estate with manicured grounds located on Linnean Avenue in Northwest Washington, DC. Duke Ellington's Main Title for the score of the motion picture *Anatomy of a Murder* was playing when they arrived.

The place was reminiscent of the twenty-five-acre Hillwood Estate, Museum and Gardens, Heiress Marjorie Merriweather Post's gift to the American people, which Norman had taken a tour of once. The tour brochure gives you the skinny:

Daughter of Charles William (C.W.) Post, inventor of the coffee substitute Postum and Grape-Nuts and Post Toasties cereals, founder of the Postum Cereal Company, a food-manufacturing empire that generated one of the largest fortunes of the early twentieth century; and former wife of Wall Street financier Edward F. Hutton, whose business acumen combined with her exceptional vision for the Postum Cereal Company, led to the creation of the General Foods Corporation, Philanthropist, socialite and art collector Marjorie Merriweather Post had been virtually American royalty, heir to two of the largest private fortunes ever amassed in the history of the United States, she was the richest woman in America.

Marjorie was possessed of a sumptuous sense of self and was obsessed with acquiring fine Sèvres porcelain and 18th-century French gold boxes; fine furnishings for her yacht *Sea Cloud* and her various properties in Palm Beach, Florida; New York; Camp Hutridge (later Topridge) in the Adirondacks; and the Hillwood Estate, repository of a world-renowned collection of eighteenth-century French decorative art and furnishings, and the most comprehensive collection of Russian imperial art outside of Russia. The collection includes Fabergé eggs, Russian porcelain, Russian Orthodox icons, Beauvais tapestries, and Sèvres porcelain, most acquired for a fraction of their value in 1937 during the turmoil of the Russian Revolution.

Whose estate was this and how the hell had he or she come by it, Blalock wondered.

The beefy middle-aged chauffer parked the limo in the circular driveway, which was a quarter acre from the public street, and then hopped out and opened the door. He stood there until they climbed out and then closed the door.

Holding one of the enormous double doors of the pristine mansion open for them, standing just inside of the doorway, was a standard issue old school, gray-headed-rickety-old-white-butler. *Jeeves*, Norman mused.

Kavitha and Norman stepped past the tuxedoed Crypt Keeper into a vast foyer with a vaulted ceiling accented by a crystal chandelier and the butler closed the door after them.

Blalock didn't bother to remove his fedora, ignoring his mother's home-training to always remove his hat when entering any home or church.

Before them, a grand double staircase rose to a second-story landing high above them. Priceless oil paintings by some of the great masters graced the walls.

"This way."

The antique butler, tremble-shuffling all the way, showed them to a...drawing room and offered them drinks. They asked for Vodka Martinis and Blalock ordered that they be shaken, not stirred.

A distinguished-looking, well-dressed Englishman entered the room carrying with both hands a sizeable wooden chest. He crossed to a large antique desk and placed the wooden box on top of it, walked over to Blalock, and extended a manicured hand. Blalock took it and the English gentleman shook his hand vigorously.

"Mr. Blalock," he grinned. "I'm Rupert Whyte. It is a pleasure to meet you, sir."

Blalock nodded. He sized up Rupert and wondered how this asshole had gotten to be such a fat cat. Was he for real or was the Brit – if he actually was a Brit – simply trying to convince him that he was a fat cat for the sake of the grift? If that was the case, then how much had this stunt set this con man back? And if so, then who the hell was that rickety old butler, his granddaddy? What was really going on, Blalock wondered.

"Please," Mr. Whyte said, gesturing, directing Norman and Kavitha to massive overstuffed red leather covered antique chairs, "Have a seat."

They sat and were devoured by the plush chairs just as the shaky old butler rattled their drinks over to them on a silver serving tray. They rescued their drinks quickly before they shook off the tray to the floor.

"Thank you," Norman and Kavitha said.

Kavitha and Norman sipped their drinks.

"Good," Norman complimented the old butler. "Shaken…"

"Not stirred," Kavitha added.

Norman flashed Kavitha a quick glance and their eyes smiled.

Mr. Whyte leaned back against the front of the massive desk and told the butler, "That will be all."

Jeeves bowed and backed away, a hitch in his step. He placed the serving tray back on the bar before exiting the room and closing the heavy wooden double doors after him.

"So, Mr. Blalock," Whyte said, "Kavitha tells me that no one knows the Folger Library better than you."

"Not alive, anyway," Blalock admitted.

Mr. Whyte smiled. "But of course, the dead are useless to me."

"The dead are useless to *everyone*," Blalock retorted. "Let's talk business. What's the deal?"

"Let's," Whyte nodded. "I am prepared to offer you one million dollars for an item you can take away from the library in your shirt pocket."

"What is it?" Blalock wanted to know.

"Shakespeare's BlackBerry," Whyte told him.

"Shakespeare's BlackBerry?"

"In the 16th Century," Whyte said, "no self-respecting Renaissance businessman would have been caught dead without a writing table, a notebook about the size of a BlackBerry, with pages covered in glue and gesso that could be written on with a metal stylus and then wiped clean with a sponge. Even Hamlet had a set. In the first act of the play, when the Danish prince learns of his father's horrible murder, the first thing he goes for are his writing tables. 'My tables,' Hamlet screams, 'meet it is I set it down!' Ergo, writer William Powers has dubbed the writing table, 'Hamlet's BlackBerry,' and used the term for the title of his book."

Blalock nodded. "I see." He sipped his drink and then continued, "So, you're saying an undiscovered writing table owned by Shakespeare, unbeknownst to the all of the experts working there, is inside the Folger vault?"

Mr. Whyte grinned and nodded. "Let me show you."

Whyte walked around to the other side of the desk and motioned to Blalock to join him. Blalock stood and walked over to the desk.

Mr. Whyte unlatched the wooden case, opened it, and removed an ornate jewelry casket. He slid the wooden box out of the way with the back of one hand and placed the jewelry box on the desk. To Blalock, the antique was reminiscent of a small scale Ark of the Covenant. It was an extraordinary piece of craftsmanship, a work of art.

Blalock fixated on it. Constructed of bronze, gilt, and silver, with a wood base, the design appeared to be the Cinquecento style of 16th Century Italy. The handle atop the casket was a golden bust of Shakespeare and the box was adorned with eight extremely detailed bronze figures of what had to be characters from the Bard's plays, and four different coats of arms rendered in gold and silver. Blalock recognized only one of the family crests: Shakespeare's.

"Magnificent," Blalock declared.

"Yes, isn't it," stated Mr. Whyte. "The wood is mulberry, cut from the same tree that stood in front of Shakespeare's family home, New Place in Stratford-upon-Avon, which he purchased in 1597." He pointed to the figures on the Cinquecento jewelry casket one at a time: "One figure on each corner. On this side, Hamlet...and Macbeth, on this side, Henry VIII...and Richard III. Two on the front, Othello...and Iago, and two on the back, King Lear...and Emilia."

"Emilia?" Dr. Blalock asked. "From Othello?"

Mr. Whyte nodded.

"Why her?" Blalock inquired. "They chose to represent only one female character, so why not...Lady Macbeth?"

"I wonder," Whyte said. "But in fact, the significance

of any of these choices eludes me."

Instead of telling Whyte he didn't believe him; Blalock simply rubbed his chin and looked at him.

"Seven years after Shakespeare's death," Whyte continued, "in the Year of Our Lord Sixteen Hundred Twenty-Three, the Herbert Brothers published Henry Condell's and John Heminge's *Mr. William Shakespeares Comedies, Histories, & Tragedies.* The profits from the First Folio and their shares in the Globe and Blackfriars theaters made Heminge and Condell wealthy men.

"Anyway, we...I learned that in the mid 1600s, Condell and Heminge commissioned a jewelry casket...a unique jewelry box with a hidden compartment." Mr. Whyte placed his hands on the ornate jewelry box. "Finally, several years ago, I located and acquired it. I detected the false bottom, but soon discovered that my search must continue.

"You see, in 1616, William Shakespeare willed to Henry Condell and John Heminge two honors each, which is roughly one pound apiece, to purchase mourning rings, a common practice in Elizabethan times. Mourning rings were worn in memory of a dead person, and bore the name, date of death, and in many instances, an image of them in any black stone, usually Jet stone. I found out I needed Condell's and Heminge's mourning rings to open the secret compartment beneath the false bottom. Let me show you."

Mr. Whyte opened the jewelry box, removed two jewelry trays one after the other, and tilted the box over onto its back. On the bottom of the box, he worked sliding wood slats, like those of a Chinese puzzle box. Subsequently, he righted the box and used a letter opener to lift the back edge of a false bottom and then with his fingers lifted it out to reveal two small cutouts of Shakespeare's profile at the bottom of the box, one on the left side and one on the right. Afterward, he removed two rings from a pocket of his suit jacket and said, "I needed these rings..."

Mr. Whyte fitted the Shakespeare cameo on one ring

into one of the cutouts and the cameo on the other ring into the other cutout. He turned the rings simultaneously, one clockwise, the other counterclockwise. He reached under the box, slid out a small drawer, removed a small object wrapped in cheesecloth, and peeled back the cloth to reveal an ornate writing table with a stylus that doubled as a latch to secure the table closed when not in use.

"This is only for dramatic effect, I'm afraid," said Mr. Whyte. "This is a prop. When I opened the secret compartment, it was empty. This box is a decoy. I learned much later you see that Condell and Heminge commissioned *two* identical jewelry boxes. The other one was recently acquired by the Folger, the one containing Shakespeare's BlackBerry."

"You *hope*," Kavitha interjected.

"Hope," Whyte said. "Yes. Hope springs eternal, my dear."

"The folks at the Folger could have found it by now," Blalock argued. "The Shakespeare Library is filled with some of the best and brightest experts on the planet."

"We will see," said Mr. Whyte. "Well? What do you say, Mr. Blalock? Are you willing to give it a go?"

The first thought that crossed Blalock's mind was why Condell and Heminge would so elaborately conceal their friend's "BlackBerry," but instead of raising the question, he simply said, "Ingenious."

Whyte nodded.

Blalock frowned and asked, "What do you hope to get out of having it? Fame or fortune?"

Whyte shrugged. "Both. You know, there are those who don't believe old Will wrote those plays and poems, who say he was actually illiterate. Imagine how important a find it would be to have absolute proof of Shakespeare's literacy."

"That's supposed to sway me?" Blalock asked. "Really? My life is at stake here, my freedom and my good name. I'd have to be a fool to go along with this."

A smile played at the right corner of Mr. Whyte's mouth. "Surely not, Dr. Blalock. Or would you prefer I call you Professor Blalock? You're not a fool; you're an historian. You got your doctorate in American History from Georgetown University at the age of 25."

Norman Blalock flushed and looked over at Kavitha, who was looking directly at him. He was startled and outraged that Mr. Whyte had invaded his privacy, but these feelings quickly faded when he considered that this rich fat cat could find out any and everything he wanted to know about anybody, everybody. He looked back at Mr. Whyte, directly into the Englishman's icy blue eyes.

"I *used* to be," Blalock countered. "In another life."

"You didn't make tenure at Howard University," Mr. Whyte argued, "and was asked to leave some 25 years ago following that scandal involving you and a teenage student, the daughter of one of the University's Trustees and chief supporters, a scandal that cost you not only a promising career, but a family. Your twins Aaron and Erin were just a few months old when your wife left you, correct? Most unfortunate. But you're still an historian and a scholar. And a collector, like Henry Clay Folger…"

"And you too it would seem," Blalock interjected. "So I'm a collector, so what? A collector is merely an organized hoarder."

"What do you owe the Folger?" Mr. Whyte snapped "You've worked there for 25 years, been passed over for promotion thrice, and now they're handing you your hat. Your pension can't hold a candle to what I'm offering you."

"Which is?"

"As I said," Mr. Whyte reminded him, "one million dollars."

Blalock snorted. "Make it two."

Mr. Whyte replied, "Let's make it three."

Blalock raised an eyebrow.

"I know all about you, Dr. Blalock," Whyte assured him. "You live in that circa 1926 Victorian rowhouse on Capitol Hill near Lincoln Park, worth roughly $1.9 million, and drive that priceless, mint-condition 1968 Jaguar XJ6 Series 1 with customized tags **PUCK**, both willed to you by your father when he passed away two years ago come…this November. I know you collect and restore antiques of all kinds. And I know you do volunteer work at a soup kitchen and never turn down the less fortunate when they ask for a handout on the street. You can do an awful lot of good with the money I'll pay you.

"I know too that you love to travel. Over the years, you've vacationed in the Caymans, Bali, Cape Verde, Ethiopia, South Africa, France, Sri Lanka, Spain, and the United Kingdom. And on and on. You're always searching for objects of rare beauty to hold, to possess. You can go on an awful lot of expeditions with that money, Dr. Blalock…and collect to your heart's content."

Blalock paused while he considered the offer. "How would payment be made?"

"We'll set up a numbered Swiss Bank account," Mr. Whyte said. "Call me from inside the Folger when you have Shakespeare's BlackBerry. You can confirm online that the payment has been deposited before you leave work and then rendezvous with me to make delivery."

"What if," Blalock said, "I open the secret compartment of the jewelry box and it's empty. What then? Surely, you're not going to pay me for nothing."

Mr. Whyte nodded. "What do you have in mind?"

"A nonrefundable deposit," Blalock said. "However this turns out, I want five hundred thousand dollars, four hundred thousand deposited in that Swiss bank you were talking about, but I want one hundred thousand dollars delivered to me personally. Fifty thousand in negotiable bearer bonds and fifty thousand in cash; five hundred one hundred dollar bills."

"Done," Mr. Whyte said. "The cash and the bearer bonds will be delivered to you tomorrow." Whyte reached into shirt pocket, removed a business card, and handed it to Blalock. "Open a numbered account at this Swiss bank and I'll deposit the four hundred thousand as soon as you give me the account number."

Blalock looked at the card and then put it into his shirt pocket. There was a long pause as Norman, his eyes glazed over, rubbed his chin, apparently staring absently in the general direction of Kavitha Netram...or was he merely gripped by lust, mesmerized by her curvaceous body and luscious legs, Whyte wondered. Whatever the case might be, Norman Blalock's attention certainly had drifted. Mr. Whyte decided to sweeten the pot and regain Blalock's full attention.

"What artifact do you most desire?" Mr. Whyte asked. "What does it for you, Dr. Blalock? Seriously, *what* is your Holy Grail?"

Norman pondered the question for a moment and then answered, "Frederick Douglass's walking stick."

The look on Mr. Whyte's face prompted Blalock to elaborate.

"When I was a young kid, in elementary school, a teacher took our class on a field trip to Cedar Hill, Frederick Douglass's home in Anacostia, Southeast. It's a National Historic Site, a museum. If you're not familiar with him, Douglass rose to prominence during the Civil War. A great thinker and scholar of his age and a staunch supporter of the abolition movement, the former slave acquired his freedom prior to the Emancipation Proclamation, became wealthy, and then had the gall to build a mansion with all the modern conveniences on a hill surrounded by all white neighbors.

"You see, at the time, black folks lived in Georgetown and white folks lived in Anacostia, you know, the working class type. You can imagine their modest existence paled by comparison to that of their rich black neighbor up on top of the hill. They were envious and bitter. It was hostile territory for Douglass. That's why Fred had cannons mounted at the four corners of his estate, aimed down the hill. The cannon mounts are still there.

"Anyway, the National Park Service tour guide made a big deal of showing us this walking stick, this cane with a white handle, made of whalebone or ivory or something exotic and expensive, I suspect.

"The tour guide gripped the handle in one hand and the wooden cane in the other, pulled them apart and revealed a sword. He waved the rapier slowly in the air as he looked at us for awhile and then said, 'This is the walking stick Mr. Douglass used whenever he took a stroll.'

"Fred wasn't going down without a fight. No, sir.

"I didn't return there until I grew up, my young children in tow. I was looking forward to seeing that walking stick again. But it wasn't there. That day I visited there when I was a kid, it had been leaning against a wall in the living room, in an area roped off from the public.

"I pulled the fresh, young tour guide to the side and inquired about the walking stick, but he had no idea what I was talking about. Evidently, someone has taken it and it hasn't even been missed. A piece of history lost." Norman paused. "I wonder where it is. I'd like to see it again. Hold it in my hand."

"Perhaps not," Mr. Whyte offered. "Perhaps it hasn't been lost. Perhaps the tour guide who showed it to you when you were a child took it when he retired. Perhaps he believed no one else would cherish it more than he. If he is no longer alive, perhaps he willed it to someone when he died...or it was sold at an estate sale. With some research, almost anything can be located...and obtained."

Blalock looked Mr. Whyte in the eye.

"Dr. Blalock," Mr. Whyte said, "I want Shakespeare's BlackBerry as much as you want Douglass's walking stick. More. Help me and I will help you."

Norman Blalock nodded slowly. "Okay, Frederick Douglass's walking stick, plus the money we talked about."

They shook hands firmly and smiled.

Leaning back in the big, overstuffed red leather chair, her lovely legs crossed at the knee, top leg slowly swinging, Kavitha smirked and sipped her drink.

Whyte was as excited as a school boy. "Describe the security."

"Well," Blalock replied, "the security personnel is top notch. The Chief of the Department of Safety and Security is Malcolm Leonard. He's a deceptively amiable, well-dressed gentleman who wears tailor made suits, but underneath he's one tough son of a bitch. Former Army Ranger, retired D.C. police captain. His second in command is new hire Nathan Rockford. Former Marine, also retired from D.C. Metropolitan Police Department, so he's no slouch.

"There are fifteen full-time and fifteen part-time special police officers employed there, not including the two top dogs, most of them with military and/or law enforcement backgrounds and several who have worked security for years.

"The library has three floors above ground and five floors underground, Alpha Deck, Beta Deck, Gamma Deck, Delta Deck, and Omega Deck. On the Delta Deck are the infirmary, a gymnasium, showers, a pistol range, an arsenal, and barracks and offices of the Armed Response Team (ART). ART also has a satellite office on the third floor down the hall from the Gundersheimer Conservation Laboratory. The office door reads, 'ART DEPT.'

"Most of the members of ART are former Navy SEALs, Rangers, Special Forces and the like.

"To present a kinder, gentler image to the public, none of the officers are armed during business hours, except for plainclothes members of ART who mingle with the visitors to exhibitions in the Great Hall. But after hours, the uniformed guards retrieve their Glock 19's from their gun lockboxes in the Security Office and strap them on. Also, uniformed members of ART are armed with MP5 submachine guns and Glock sidearms and conduct random roving patrols of the entire facility. Oh, and hidden at Central, there are two guns accessible to security personnel during business hours. Just in case. And we've got MPD and Capitol Police for back-up.

"As for the physical and technological security measures, the vault was manufactured by the Mosler Safe Company out of Cincinnati, which was founded in the mid 1860's. Prior to WWII, Mosler installed several vaults in Hiroshima's Mitsui Bank building. The vaults survived 'Little Boy,' one of the atom bombs America dropped on Japan to end World War II. Later, the company also manufactured doors for U.S. nuclear missile silos.

"There is a time lock on the vault, and to gain access to the vault door on the Beta Deck through a sliding bullet-resistant glass door rated to withstand multiple impacts from .50 caliber rounds, biometric verification of persons authorized to access the vault via facial and voice recognition software, and palm and retinal scanners, all supplied and maintained by BioSec Systems, Inc. Monday – Saturday, a guard has to be present at 8:45 am when the time lock disengages and the curator inputs the combination and opens the vault door and a guard has to be present when the vault door is closed and locked at 4:45 pm and the time lock is set.

"Digital cameras supplied and maintained by Horus Security, Inc., are all over the building, their recorded images stored forever offsite, time and date stamped, always retrievable for review. One of them is aimed at the vault door 24/7. Monitors are at Central, which is the Guard's Desk in the west lobby, in the offices of ART, and in the Security Office, where images cannot only be monitored, but retrieved and reviewed onsite via a Horus Wadjit EX 9000 Series Digital Video Recorder.

"The Folger has a water fire suppression system only in the Elizabethan Theatre since water presents as much of a danger as fire to the books, manuscripts and artwork. Therefore, Halon Fire Extinguishing Systems are in place to protect the collection. Since Halon is deadly to humans, plans are in place to replace the Halon Systems with an alternative fire extinguishing system, possibly with DuPont's FE-13 gaseous extinguishing agent.

"The most valuable books are chipped, like clothing and shoes in department stores. Take them out through either the Visitors' Entrance or the Research Entrance and an alarm in the vestibule of that entrance sounds. There are also body scanners in the vestibules, like airports use. Bring in a gun or a knife and the alarm sounds."

Whyte whistled. He paused and then asked, "When do you think you can get at the box?"

Blalock rubbed his chin. "It's difficult to say. I'm pretty sure I can circumvent the security measures, but beforehand I have to do recon in the vault to find out exactly where the jewelry box is. The less time in the vault, the greater my chances of pulling off the job. Give me…a couple of weeks to get the lay of the land."

"Fine," Whyte said. "Keep me posted."

Blalock nodded and then stared at the ornate jewelry casket. Without looking at Mr. Whyte, he said, "I'll need a burner with your phone number preprogrammed into it…"

"A burner?" Whyte asked

"You know, a ghost phone," Blalock answered. "An untraceable and disposable cell phone, preferably a 4G iPhone. I don't want records of phone calls to *either* of you on my personal cell phone. If I need anything else, I'll let you know."

Mr. Whyte nodded. "Done."

[0000]

Blalock rose early on the morning of September 14th. He had a doctor's appointment that morning, but he needed to get dinner started, the leftovers of which he'd take to work for lunch the following day. He also wanted to surf the Internet before he left.

Norman showered, brushed his teeth, and got dressed and then went to the kitchen.

Bruno underfoot, Norman diced six slices of bacon and tossed them into a hot skillet. He cut 3 medium carrots and 3 medium potatoes into 1-inch pieces, and diced 3 cloves of garlic. He combined 1/4 cup all-purpose flour; 1/2 teaspoon salt and 1/2 teaspoon freshly ground black pepper, and then cut 2 pounds of boneless lamb shoulder into 1-inch pieces. He dredged the lamb cubes in the flour mixture, removed the cooked bacon from the skillet, and then browned the lamb in the same skillet. He removed the lamb and set it aside and then deglazed the skillet with 1 cup of beef broth and 1 cup of white wine. He put the lamb and the wine/broth mixture into his Crock Pot, added the carrots, potatoes, garlic, 2 whole bay leaves, and 1 teaspoon of dried thyme, and stirred the stew. He put the lid on the Crock Pot and turned it to **LOW**. Voilà! Dinner was on. He'd enjoy his lamb stew that evening with a bottle of Chalone Pinot Noir 2006, he was sure. He wasn't allowed to eat before the test he was scheduled for that morning, so he had to skip breakfast.

Norman put two cups of dog food into Bruno's dish and then sat at the dining room table. He opened and turned on his laptop and then researched Shakespeare on the Internet while Bruno chomped his breakfast.

Whyte's story didn't sit right with Blalock. Something was missing, something Whyte wasn't going to tell him; something Whyte needed to conceal. That's what his gut was telling him anyway.

Norman started with the coats of arms on the jewelry casket he hadn't recognized. He'd committed them to memory. All he needed to do was search for family crests by name and see what came up. He searched the Internet until it was time to leave for his doctor's appointment.

Norman arrived at the Clinton Radiology Associates located on Piscataway Road in Clinton, Maryland on time for his 8:30 appointment to undergo a nuclear stress test his doctor had ordered when he'd visited him the week before. During that appointment, his doctor had also told him that his A1-C and cholesterol levels were atrocious and had upped the milligrams for his daily doses of Crestor and Glipizide and ordered him to stick to the diet he'd prescribed at his last visit.

He filled out some paperwork, signed a consent form, and then was taken into a small room where a fat middle-aged Latina Cardiology Tech/Nurse told him to take off his shirt and tee shirt. He complied and then she stuck a needle in his right arm and started an IV, and through it gave him his first injection of Cardiolite, a nuclear radioactive isotope. She left him alone in the room for 45 minutes to let the Cardiolite circulate to his heart.

When the waiting period was over, a pretty African American Nuclear Medicine Tech came in and took him to another room where she directed him to lay on his back on a table with his hand behind his head and ordered him to remain still while a camera moved about him, scanning and taking pictures for 15 minutes.

Following the completion of the scan, he was escorted by the fat Latina to a stress testing room. The Cardio Tech/Nurse had him lay on a stretcher while she hooked him up to equipment. She then attached a bag of saline to his IV. The nurse abraded his chest with alcohol and a cloth and attached ten electrode patches to his chest and torso. Afterward, she attached wires to the electrodes in order to monitor his heart rate and EKG to record his resting EKG and blood pressure. When the readings were recorded, a cardiologist came into the room.

"Good morning, Mr. Blalock. I'm Dr. Nazemian."

"Good morning."

Dr. Nazemian directed Norman to stand, making sure to be careful with the electrodes and the wires connected to him, and to get on a treadmill nearby.

"Mr. Blalock, the treadmill will start off slowly and then gradually increase in speed. For the last few minutes, it will slow for a few minutes to the start-up speed for a cooldown period and then the treadmill will stop. You'll be running for 20 minutes."

Blalock nodded.

The treadmill started off slowly, just as the doctor said. When it started picking up speed, Norman said, "Colonel Steve Austin, a man barely alive. We can rebuild him; make him better than he was before. Better. Stronger. Faster."

Norman exaggerated the movements of his arms to simulate running in slow motion, like Lee Majors as Steve Austin, and then hummed the theme to the popular 70s TV show, The Six Million Dollar Man.

The doctor and the nurse were in stitches.

Twenty minutes later, breathless and sweat-drenched, Norman climbed down off the treadmill. He huffed, "Thanks…for…showing…me…a…great…time."

"We're not done yet," said Dr. Nazemian. "Have a seat here on the bed."

Norman complied. The nurse removed the ten electrode patches.

"Now you have to go back to the other room so we can scan you again," Dr. Nazemian told him, "but first you need to drink some water. Nurse Pineda will take you. When we're done, she will show you to where you can freshen up and get dressed. I won't see you again today, but your doctor will give you the test results in a few days. Take care, Mr. Blalock."

Norman nodded and shuffled out behind Nurse Pineda.

That evening, Blalock had just finished listening to a voice message his doctor left on his cell phone urging him to come in ASAP to discuss his test results and the treatment for heart disease he should undergo immediately when his doorbell rang. His dog Bruno, who was chained in his backyard, started barking. He opened the door and found Kavitha Netram wearing black silk stockings and a form-fitting short red dress with matching three-inch stilettos, a big black leather hand bag hanging from a strap over her left shoulder, long raven hair draped down her back. As always, she smelled of expensive shampoo, body wash, lotion, and perfume…and of something sweeter still: youth.

"Do you have a dog?" she asked.

"Yeah," he said. "He's in the backyard."

"Sounds big," she said.

"He is," he assured her.

"Nice house," said Kavitha. "It looks like a castle."

"Well, a man's home is his castle," Norman quipped. "I don't remember giving you my address."

She gave him a you-should-know-better look and ignored his statement.

"You weren't at work today," Kavitha protested. "Having second thoughts?"

Blalock shook his head. "I had a doctor's appointment."

"You didn't tell me," she pouted.

"I don't have to tell you anything. You're not my girlfriend, Kavitha."

She leaned her supple young body against his, placed her right hand lightly on his chest, then looked doe-eyed up at him and whispered, "I *could* be."

Kavitha lifted herself on tiptoes, laid a wet kiss on his chin, and then purred, "Let me in, Splenda Daddy. I've got

your booty. You know, your loot, here in my bag."
Norman pulled her inside and slammed the door.

[0000]

Later that night, the soothing tones of the Miles Davis Quintet performing *My Funny Valentine* emanating from his vintage TEAC reel-to-reel in his living room, glasses of Chalone Pinot Noir 2006 and bowls of what remained of Blalock's Rustic Lamb Stew in front of them, Blalock, wearing his black Nautica robe, sat at his antique dining table across from Kavitha, who was wearing his souvenir *Hawk 'n' Dove Last Call* tee shirt and nothing more. The tee shirt had never looked better...and never would again, Norman was sure. Umpf. Those breasts. Those legs. Those eyes. Those lips. Those thighs. Those hips...
Lust sees with the eyes, not the mind, he mused.
Kavitha rubbed her flat belly and announced, "I'm stuffed. My compliments to the chef."
Norman nodded.
Blalock's dog Bruno laid on the floor next to Kavitha, his belly exposed, begging for affection. Kavitha rubbed his belly and his eyes rolled up into his head.
"This is the friendliest big dog I've ever seen," Kavitha observed.
"Bruno's a ladies' man," said Blalock.
Kavitha said, "I see. Hey, why did you see your doctor today?"
Norman shrugged. "Just a check-up. I'm fine."
She smiled and nodded. "Yes you are. Oh. Clear an area here on the table."
Norman complied and moved the bowls, wine bottle, and glasses to one side of the dining table.
Kavitha stopped rubbing Bruno and he rolled over and stood up. He nuzzled her left breast.
"I'm going to have my hands full," she said.

"Go away, Bruno," Norman ordered. Bruno trotted away a few feet and then sat down. He kept his eyes on Kavitha, remaining vigilant for more affection.

"How long have you had him?" she asked.

"Three years," Norman said. "Well, actually he's really my father's dog. Dino was my dog. He was a German Shepherd/Rottweiler/Pit Bull/Black Lab Mix I got when he was a newborn puppy. He was thorough, he was about his business. Bruno is just a good watchdog. He barks loud and plays a good bluffing game like he's vicious, but he'd just try to lick a burglar to death if one got in.

"Pops got Bruno from an animal shelter a year before he died. They told him at the shelter that the dog was seven months old, but when Pops took him to the vet for his shots, the vet told him that Bruno was probably around four months old. The vet opened his mouth and pointed out, 'Look at all these baby teeth.' Hell, he weighed over fifty pounds then.

"On top of that, that damned dog has some kind of allergies. I have to give him prescription drugs. His last vet visit cost me $282. And on top of that, I have to feed him nothing but all-natural *Blue Buffalo* dog food, which is fifty dollars for a 30-pound bag. The vet thinks he may be allergic to the preservatives in dog food!"

"He's a sweetheart," Kavitha said. "He's worth every penny and you know it. Stop trying to talk tough; you love this dog. Love shows. Look at how well-kept he is, how healthy and well-adjusted he is. Look at his shiny black coat; look at how well he behaves. Dogs reflect their owners. This *was* your father's dog, but he's yours now. He's spoiled too. *You* did that."

Norman opened his mouth to protest, but Kavitha cut him off before he could utter a word.

"Anyway," she said as she picked up her big, black leather hand bag off the floor, unzipped it, and emptied it onto the table. Negotiable bearer bonds, stacks of $100 bills, and a cell phone and its accessories (wall and car chargers and USB cable) tumbled out. She picked up the cell phone and handed it to him. "The iPhone you asked for preprogrammed per your request."

He took the phone and laid it on the table, never taking his eyes from the stacks of cold, hard cash.

"Thanks."

A gleam in his eyes, his lower lip subtly trembling, Norman Blalock began to count his money.

Kavitha stood and stretched, hiking up the tiny tee shirt she almost wore, which Blalock *did* take notice of. She sashayed over to the other side of the room.

"How did you end up at the Folger?" she wanted to know.

"Fate," he told her. "When Howard U dumped me, I was out on my ass. I got into security, did a couple of gigs, and then stumbled upon the Folger when a coworker told me he was applying for a security job there. I applied too. I got the job, he didn't.

"Like my other gigs, I just showed them my high school diploma."

She turned and looked at him. "You didn't want them to contact Howard U, of course. No sterling recommendations to be found there.

"That's why you were passed over for promotion. You needed at least a bachelor's degree to qualify for the positions, but they think you're just a high school graduate."

Norman nodded. "Better that than them learning the truth."

"And what is the truth?" Kavitha asked.

Distracted by Kavitha, he finally, gave up trying to count his loot.

"I'm a person of disreputable character," Norman confessed.

They both fell silent for awhile.

"Thank you," he said. "And thank Mr. Whyte for me."

Kavitha looked him directly in the eye. "You're talking about the money, right?"

"Thank him for *everything*," Blalock said flatly.

"He didn't tell me to screw you, Norm, if that's what you're thinking. That was *my* idea; I did that on my own."

"Can he?" Norm wanted to know. "Can he command you? Will you do a*nyone* he says?"

"Screw you," Kavitha spat. "I'm nobody's whore, Norm, not Rupert Whyte's, not yours, not anyone's."

"I apologize," Norm said. "I'm just trying to figure out the nature of your relationship with..."

"Well, then bloody ask!" she hissed.

"Okay, Kavitha. Okay. I just want to know who everybody is. Okay? What's up with you two?"

"He is my employer, nothing more," Kavitha said calmly. "Our relationship is strictly business. Besides, the bugger doesn't even like women."

"And what business is that?"

Low in the background, emanating from the reel-to-reel in the living room, Astrud Gilberto and Stan Getz performing *The Girl from Ipanema* began to play before she responded.

With a twinkle in her dark, soul-piercing eyes and a smile playing at the corner of her mouth, she glared at him and said, "Crime."

"Big time," Norm added.

Kavitha nodded and her long, dark hair swung gently forward and back. "Big time crime. High stakes crime." She waved her hand toward the table full of loot and added, "That's where the money is. Not teaching. Not law enforcement. Not security."

Norm smiled. "Okay, Junior."

Kavitha smiled. "Okay, Splenda Daddy."

They laughed.

After a few moments had passed, Norman looked at Kavitha and asked, "How long have you known about me?"

"What?" she asked.

"About my shameful act of infidelity that cost me my career, my marriage, and my family."

Kavitha looked uncomfortable and did not reply.

"You knew all about me right from the start, as soon as you decided I was the perfect candidate for this inside job you dug up all of the dirt...long before you approached me at the Hawk 'n' Dove. Didn't you?"

Finally, Kavitha nodded and said, "Yes, Norman."

Norman nodded and said, "I thought so. You knew my girlfriend had left me too. That's why you felt comfortable in coming here."

They both fell silent.

Kavitha broke the silence. "It's not personal, Norm. Checking you out was just standard operating procedure. Mr. Whyte needs to know who he's working with..."

"And so do you," Norman interjected.

"Yes," Kavitha admitted. "So do I."

"So do we all," said Norman.

They both fell silent.

Kavitha broke the silence again. "Want to tell me about it?"

"About what?" asked Norman.

"The girl," Kavitha said.

Norman sighed. After awhile, he said, "The girl was one of my students. Her father, Richard Daye, was on the Board of Trustees. When he found out about the affair, he was furious. I had soiled his precious flower. He'd wanted to kill me, he said, but instead threatened that if I didn't resign he'd have me charged with statutory rape..."

"She was underage?" Kavitha interrupted.

"No, she was an adult," Norman answered.

Kavitha looked at him sideways and asked, "*How* much of an adult?"

Norman sighed. "Eighteen."

"Eighteen," said Kavitha. "Well, that's not

illegal…it's just barely legal is what it is. But she was an adult, yeah. So, how could her father threaten you with a sex crime? Or was the allegation true after all? How old was she when the affair *began*? Never mind, don't answer that. And you were how old?"

"Twenty-five," said Norman.

"So," Kavitha said, "what happened was, you couldn't survive with the stigma associated with being a suspected pedophile – that's the kiss of death for a school teacher – so you resigned to avoid the publicity. But the trustee wasn't satisfied with just your resignation; he screwed you royally by leaking the allegation to your community. And you lost everything. Is that the way of it?"

Norman shrugged and said, "He wanted to ruin my career and destroy me and that did the trick. Whatever works.

"The bottom line is that the whole mess was my own fault. I let my ex-wife Rita down, I let my children down, I let myself down. I let *everybody* down. I was the golden boy with a promising future, I was a man with a plan. I was going to change the world one class at a time. But I failed. I lost sight of what was important to me and I failed. If I had stayed my course, stayed true to my promise, I would not have touched that girl and incurred the wrath of Richard Daye and I'd have lived my life the way I had planned. As close to the plan as possible, anyway."

"It's not too late, Norm. You can still make a difference. You're about to come into a large sum of money. Money changes everything."

Kavitha looked at him for a few moments and then raised her glass and made a toast: "To whatever works."

Norman raised his glass and agreed, "To whatever works."

They drank and then fell silent again.

Abruptly, Kavitha changed the subject. "Hey, Fred, Gary, Luther, Helen, and Tanya were telling me Folger ghost stories today."

"Which ones?" he asked.

"Let's see," she said. "Helen told me about the time she was working the midnight shift and started dozing and all of a sudden, books in the gift shop flew from the shelves and hit the floor. She suspects it was the Folgers telling her to stay awake and guard their stuff."

Norman laughed and so did Kavitha.

You got any ghost stories...Splenda Daddy."

They laughed again.

After they composed themselves, she asked again. "Well, do you?"

"A couple," he admitted.

"Well, tell me a good one," she demanded.

"Okay," he said. "I was working the midnight shift with a brand new guard – I can't recall his name at the moment. Anyway, I left the new guy at the desk for a minute. He called me over the air, sounding frantic, and requested that I respond to Central. When I got there, he claimed that an old white man with a beard, wearing a fedora and a trench coat like Bogart, walked passed him at Central, said goodnight, and walked straight out the front door. Everyone was supposed to have left for the day, all long gone, so I made sure the front door was locked, and then told him to come on, we're going to search the building.

"During the search, the new guy froze in front of the portrait of Henry Clay Folger in the Old Reading Room, you know, near Mr. and Mrs. Folger's columbarium niche. He pointed at the painting and yelled, 'That's him! That's him!'

"That's *who*?" I asked.

"'Him!' the new guy yelled. 'The man who just left! That's him!'

"He quit on the spot and left the building."

They laughed for quite awhile and then they sat there silently for awhile to catch their breath.

Finally, Kavitha asked him, "Do you believe in ghosts, Norm?"

Low in the background, emanating from the reel-to-reel in the living room, Mark Isham performed Main Title from *The Cooler*.

Blalock took a deep breath and considered the question before he answered, "I don't know, Kavitha. Sometimes, maybe. How about you?"

Kavitha smiled. "I don't know. Sometimes, maybe. But I figured you'd have more insight; you *have* been working in a tomb for twenty-five years, Dr. Blalock."

Norman smiled. "Well, Dr. Netram, I do not have special insight. The dead don't concern me; it's the living I'm worried about. Dead people can't do me any harm."

Kavitha kept smiling. "Uh huh. You know you're afraid of the Folgers."

Norman laughed. "Yeah, right."

Kavitha got up, walked over to Norman, and took his face in her hands. "It's me you'd better be afraid of, Dr. Blalock."

"I *am* afraid of you, Dr. Netram."

Kavitha giggled, sat in his lap, and sweetly kissed him on the lips.

[0000]

Later still that night while Kavitha was sleeping, Norman slipped out of bed, took his loot from the dining table, and crept to the basement where he threw back the tablecloth covering his antique floor safe situated in a far corner, dialed in the combination, opened its door and stashed his booty. He spun the dial, put the tablecloth back in place, and returned to bed.

Kavitha Netram nestled against him, Norman slept deeply, peacefully. He dreamed of a plethora of scantily clad women dancing like music video sluts, Kavitha in the center,

Palm trees gently swaying in the background. Norm, topped with a Fedora, wearing Ray-Ban shades, a charcoal gray Firado suit with a red Salvatore Ferragamo tie and matching kerchief crisply folded and peeking from his breast pocket, an 18kt Yellow Gold Diamond Rolex Oyster Perpetual, and black and gray Moretti shoes, was front and center stage, chomping on a fat Havana tucked in the corner of his mouth. Cash in one manicured hand, a Gin and Juice cocktail in the other, he bounced and swayed as Snoop Dogg laid down his megahit *Gin and Juice* in the background. All night long, it seemed, Blalock's backup dancers and he bounced and swayed to the beat of the music, the baseline thumping deep in the center of his chest, of his very being.

"Rollin down the street, smoking ENDO, sipping on Gin and juice

[Laid Back] with my mind on my money and my money on my mind!

"Rollin down the street, smoking ENDO, sipping on Gin and juice

[Laid Back] with my mind on my money and my money on my mind..."

[0000]

The next morning when Norman woke, Kavitha was gone. He wasn't offended; he was too grateful. He felt great! He didn't even mind Bruno waking him up to feed him at around 4:30, as usual, by resting one of his boxing glove-sized paws on his chest.

On the drive to work, *Gin and Juice* by Snoop Dogg came over the airwaves.

Norman laughed and yelled, "Hey!"

He turned the volume way up and, bouncing and swaying to the beat, rapped along. He never noticed the motorists in other vehicles staring at him.

"Rollin down the street, smoking ENDO, sipping on Gin and juice

[Laid Back] with my mind on my money and my money on my mind!

"Rollin down the street, smoking ENDO, sipping on Gin and juice

[Laid Back] with my mind on my money and my money on my mind..."

Norman Blalock arrived at work early; 0700 hours when he wasn't due in until 0800, and parked his mint-condition black 1968 Jaguar XJ6 with personalized tags **PUCK** in Puck Circle. Upbeat and happy, he exited the car and closed the door after him. Quickly, with pep in his step, swinging his fabric-constructed insulated navy blue colored lunchbox containing leftover lamb stew, a couple of slices of baguette, and a bottle of Chocolate Muscle Milk, he strode up the stairs like a man with purpose and then swung open and walked through the double outer doors of Door 49, into the vestibule, and through the oak and glass inner double doors into the west lobby.

"How's it going, Helen?" he asked the guard at Central.

"Fine, Norm," SPO Rowe replied.

"Good," said Norman.

Blalock whistled as he walked through the archway into the west hallway restricted to authorized personnel, turned left and proceeded down the stairs to the Security Office. He walked in, past the smiling face of the late, great SPO Luther Wayne Chaney hanging in a wood picture frame on the wall to Norman's left. Captain Rockford was there when Blalock entered the office.

"Good morning, captain."

"Call me Rocky. Good morning."

"Anything special going on today, Rocky?"

"No," Rocky answered. "Business as usual."

"How about I arrange for Betsy Walsh to give you a tour of the vault today after I give you the grand tour?"

"Sounds good," Rocky said. "Set it up."

"Will do, Rocky."

Rocky left the office.

Blalock smiled.

Norman, Rocky, and Kavitha assembled in the west lobby at 0900 hours.

Captain Rockford leered at Kavitha and licked his lips. "Did I tell you already what a pleasure it is to meet you, young lady?"

"Yes," Kavitha said, "you did, captain."

"Call me Rocky," he grinned.

"I understand you're retired MPD, like the chief," Blalock said.

"That's right," Captain Rockford replied. "Twenty-seven years, retired as a captain. Before that, I was a marine, two tours, left with the rank of lieutenant. You ever in the military?"

Norman shook his head and said, "No."

"That's too bad," said the captain. "Military service really makes a man out of you."

Lt. Blalock looked at Captain Rockford for a time and

then said, "Okay, let's start in the Great Hall."

Captain Rockford and Kavitha followed Lt. Blalock into the exhibition hall.

Captain Rockford eyeballed Kavitha. "You an Indian or something?"

"I'm British," Kavitha said.

"Okay," the captain said. "I love your accent."

"Thank you," Kavitha said.

"The Folger Shakespeare Library," Lt. Blalock said, "is a private research library designed by noted architect Paul Philippe Cret. Although it was initially instituted to assist Shakespeare scholars, more scholars apply for Readers Cards to be permitted to use the library to conduct Renaissance-period-based research than do Shakespearean researchers. According to the Folger website, the library has more than 256,000 books; 60,000 manuscripts; 250,000 playbills; 200 oil paintings; some 50,000 drawings, watercolors, prints, and photographs; and a wealth of other materials, including musical instruments, costumes, and films.

"The library was founded by Industrialist Henry Clay Folger and his wife Emily. Ground was broken for the library and the cornerstone laid in 1930, shortly before Henry Folger's death in June of the same year, and it was dedicated on Shakespeare's birthday, April 23, 1932. The dedication ceremony was attended by the ambassadors to France, Germany and Great Britain, and President and Mrs. Herbert Hoover."

"Folgers, the coffee people?" Captain Rockford asked.

"No," Lt. Blalock replied. "Although the coffee people are distant cousins. Henry Folger was the President of Standard Oil. Apparently, his obsession with the First Folio began when he heard Ralph Waldo Emerson give a lecture at Amherst College in 1879."

Blalock told them about how the Folgers chose the site of the library when they walked around Washington during a ravel delay and how their original plan to erect the library as an Elizabethan style structure met with opposition as it would clash with the architecture of the federal government buildings surrounding it. Therefore, the building is neoclassical on the outside and Elizabethan style on the inside.

"This is the Great Hall," said Blalock. "Our current exhibition is *Manifold Greatness: The Life and Afterlife of the King James Bible*, which includes a bible once owned by Frederick Douglass, purchased from his estate by Elvis Presley."

Kavitha flashed Norman a knowing smile.

"One of the institution's 82 First Folios," Norman continued, "is on permanent display, so at this time, the two most influential books in the English language – the King James Bible and Shakespeare's First Folio – are on display together for the first time."

He pointed out the Great Seal of the United States above the west side entrance into the Great Hall and the coat of arms of England above the east side entrance.

"Note the motto below the coat of arms of Great Britain, 'Dieu Et Mon Droit.'

"That sounds like French," Captain Rockford said.

"Yes it is," Lt. Blalock said, "but during that period, Norman French was the language of the Royal Court."

"I see," said Captain Rockford.

"Roughly translated," Blalock offered, "it means 'God and my right' or 'My divine right.'"

"The divine right of kings," Kavitha chimed in.

Blalock looked her in the eye and nodded, a smile playing at the corner of his mouth. He looked at his Seiko. "Kavitha, since you're already familiar with the Elizabethan Theatre, what say I show you around some more another time? I'd like to familiarize the captain with our security measures."

"Sure, no problem," she said. "I'll catch you later."

Kavitha Netram turned and walked away.

"See you, Kavitha," the captain said after her. He watched her until she left the Great Hall. "Lord, have mercy."

"This way, captain…"

"Rocky," Captain Rockford said. "Call me Rocky."

"I'll show you the box office, give you the code, and then familiarize you with Delta and Omega Decks, and the biometric security protocols. Then we'll stop by to see the department head of IT, Mary Bloodworth. She'll program the voice, facial, retinal, and palm and fingerprint recognition software so the system will grant you access to secure areas."

Captain Rockford nodded. "Sounds good."

[0000]

After Norman gave Rocky the grand tour of the lower decks, he took him to Beta Deck to meet Betsy Walsh, the head of Reader Services, who had been at the Folger for some 40 years. There he ran into Curator of Art Erin Blake, Rare Materials Cataloger Nadia Seiler, and Reference Assistant Camille Seerattan and introduced them to Captain Rockford.

Betsy took Norm and Rocky on a 45 minute private tour of the vault, beginning at 0930 hours. As always, Blalock was fascinated by the treasures stored there. On the other hand, Rocky looked bored.

Blalock and Rocky saw several of the many volumes of Shakespeare First Folios and all manner of Shakespeareana, and a plethora of books, manuscripts, and objects d'art from the English Renaissance as far back as the 15th Century.

What Blalock did not see in the Babette Craven Art Vault is the twin Cinquecento style jewelry casket.

[0000]

Weeks passed before he got his break, but he spent the time researching Condell and Heminge, writing tables, and the coats of arms on the 16th Century casket; and just kickin' it with Kavitha, spending several nights just sitting around at home smoking marijuana and listening to music from his vast and eclectic collection and talking and laughing or eating popcorn and other munchies while they watched films from his extensive collection, Bruno always nearby.

Kavitha had seemed to enjoy some of his favorite films noir, including ***The Postman Always Rings Twice***; ***Gilda***, ***Out of the Past***, ***Double Indemnity***; ***To Have and Have Not***, ***The Big Sleep***, ***The Maltese Falcon***; ***Casablanca***; ***Dark Passage***, ***Citizen Kane***; Alfred Hitchcock's ***Notorious***, ***Vertigo***, and ***Psycho***; ***Scarlet Street***, ***Sunset Boulevard***, and ***Body Heat***. She seemed to have enjoyed all of the films he'd shown her in fact and had been attentive as he'd given her his take on each movie, even when he'd raved once about the genius of film score composer Bernard Herrmann…and even when he'd explained to her that the MacGuffin is a plot device that gives the protagonist and/or antagonist a goal or object to pursue that drives the story she'd listened intently as though she was interested in the fact that the MacGuffin in ***The Maltese Falcon*** *is* the Maltese Falcon and that Hitchcock was the master of the MacGuffin. And so on.

She'd appeared to be interested in *everything* he had to say in fact. It was as if she hung on his every word…

Conversely, he could not get into the Bollywood hits she raved about as she made him sit through them. Sure, the women are beautiful and the music and the dancing is wonderful, but Norman needed more than that from a movie.

He'd taken her out on several dates as well. He'd taken her to all the tourist attractions, all of the museums, memorials and monuments, all of the points of interest in the Washington metropolitan area. He'd taken her out to breakfast, lunch, and dinner. He'd taken her to several movies and to various Jazz clubs in and around D.C., including *Blues Alley* in Georgetown and the *Bohemian Caverns* on 11th Street, NW. They'd seen Joe Sample at *Blues Alley* and Gerald Albright at the *Bohemian Caverns*. He'd even taken her to the Washington National Opera at the John F. Kennedy Center for the Performing Arts to see Claudio Monteverdi's *L'Orfeo*. They not only enjoyed the performance, but they enjoyed making fun of the other patrons.

Among the patrons was one particular decked-out cougar with her boy toy in tow. Norman nudged Kavitha, directed her attention toward the couple, and whispered, "Norma Desmond."

Without missing a beat, Kavitha pulled off a more than fair impression of Gloria Swanson as she glares at the camera at the end of **Sunset Boulevard** and hisses, "Alright, Mr. DeMille, I'm ready for my close-up!"

It was a hoot!

He'd even taken her for a tour of his hero Frederick Douglass's estate, Cedar Hill, located about a mile from Capitol Hill in the Anacostia Historic District, Mecca for DC's working class.

He told Kavitha that in the 19th Century, due to the need to provide housing for the many new employees working at the Washington Navy Yard on the other side of the Anacostia River, the initially predominantly white working-class neighborhood of Anacostia was created in 1818, generally consisting of two-story brick and wood frame structures, mostly in the Italianate, Cottage, and Washington Row House architectural styles, but also including a few Queen Anne and Cottage style homes. In 1877, Frederick Douglass bought Cedar Hill, the estate belonging to John Van Hook, one of the developers of Uniontown, the whites-only neighborhood among the first suburbs in the District of Columbia. Douglass lived at Cedar Hill until his death in 1895.

In 1854, John Van Hook and his partners in the Union

Land Association, John Dobler and John Fox, bought up land at the intersection of Nichols Avenue and Good Hope Road and laid out Uniontown. Particularly appealing to the white Navy Yard workers was the clause in the contract forbidding "negroes, mulattoes, pigs, or soap boiling." The embodiment of white working class resentment towards free blacks, Uniontown existed in an uneasy coexistence of a substantial German immigrant population of small landowners and tenant farmers; well-off working and middle class communities for free blacks in Stantontown and along Good Hope Road; and wealthy slaveholders and their slaves. After the Civil War, thousands of other blacks immigrated to the District and the black population tripled in one decade.

Kavitha also loved fast cars. One weekend, they left early on a Saturday morning and took his mint-condition black '68 Jaguar XJ6 Series 1 out on the open road where he could open up his baby **PUCK**'s 4.2 L straight six-cylinder, manual transmission engine.

They took **PUCK** out on Skyline Drive, the 105-mile roadway that runs the entire length of the Shenandoah National Park in the Blue Ridge Mountains of Virginia. Skyline Drive is very popular in the fall when the leaves are changing colors, attracting over two million motorists annually. They drove on Skyline Drive the whole day, stayed overnight at the Residence Inn in Waynesboro, Virginia on Saturday, and then got back out on the open road early Sunday morning and headed back to D.C. The whole time, they listened to gems from his eclectic music collection that he'd burned to CDs. (Her personal favorite tune on the road had been the fitting and infectious *Skyline Drive* by Shahin & Sepehr). And while they were in their hotel room, they listened to his music via his iPod and Bose SoundDock Series II Digital Music System. His iPod contained some 2,500 tunes.

Norman drove up Skyline Drive and Kavitha drove back. She giggled all the way home.

All the while, he never let on once that he was ailing, nor did he return the numerous phone calls from his doctor's office. In fact, he'd become foolhardy and started smoking cigarettes again as well after more than a decade of abstinence, thanks to Kavitha. He hadn't even known she was a smoker until one night after knee-buckling sex she pulled a pack of cigarettes from her Coach bag, lit up an elegant cigarette rolled in black paper with a gold colored filter and offered him one, which he readily accepted and blissfully smoked. He didn't have a clue; she never once smelled of cigarette smoke. The sweet smell of youth and top-shelf beauty products overpowered the scent of tobacco, he supposed.

It bothered him that he had not volunteered his services to the So Others Might Eat (SOME) soup kitchen located on the unit block of O Street, NW during the entire time he'd been hanging out with Kavitha, because Norman did not attend church and this was his way of keeping the faith. He believed in God but he did not believe in religion.

Norman increased his donations to SOME to compensate for his absence...and to assuage his guilty conscience. To that end, he'd also increased handing out money to the homeless he encountered.

Norman's break finally came on the afternoon of Friday, October 28th. Safety Team members and security personnel were called to the art vault, where an overhead pipe had sprung a leak and the spraying water was putting objects d'art at immediate risk.

Lt. Blalock ran to the art vault to find water spraying from the ruptured overhead pipe and SPO Helen Rowe and SPO Fred Baylor, along with Head of Conservation Renate Mesmer and staff members who worked in the vault, frantically moving heavy cardboard boxes, paintings, and objects d'art out of harm's way, while Facilities Manager David Conine, Building Services Supervisor Keith Johnson, and Chief Engineer Mitchell supervised building services technicians and specialists who worked frantically to cut off the flow of water. Building Services Technician Specialist Berhane Fessehaye was the front man, working directly on the hole in the pipe, with Reggie Young, Huston Jenkins, and Gregory Pendleton backing him up, taking turns twisting the stuck emergency water shut-off valve to the closed position. Blalock sprang into action, grabbing items and moving them to safety and, like the rest of the team, turned back immediately to grab and move more items.

Finally, the shower subsided, after everything was out of harm's way. Soaking wet and tired, the team caught its breath.

As the experts discussed the procedure for transporting the wet objects d'art upstairs to the Conservation Lab for damage assessment and restoration, something on a far shelf caught Blalock's eye, something gleaming, elaborate, and magnificent. And it hadn't gotten wet. It must have already been out of harm's way when the pipe sprang a leak. But it hadn't been there when Betsy gave them the tour. He realized that the jewelry casket must have been in the Conservation Lab and must have been returned to the vault after Betsy gave Rocky and him the tour. Of course. That was it.

Following a meeting of the Safety and Security Committee held immediately after the disaster, Chief Leonard, at the direction of Director Michael Witmore, had ordered that security personnel working each shift check the art vault for leaks once per hour over the next few days until repair parts that had been ordered arrived and were install. After hours, security was to use the emergency back way into the vault. Perfect.

Blalock's mind was reeling. Now he knew the location of the twin jewelry casket and had justification for being in the vault. Now all he had to do was go inside, crack open the casket, and pluck out Shakespeare's BlackBerry. That's all he had to do. However, he had to do it ASAP because Captain Rockford in that same meeting had pointed out that the Vault Emergency Entrance Protocol was flawed. His plan to retrofit a few more door locks with biometric systems and have cameras installed in the vault area had been approved on the spot. Once these upgrades were made and the damaged pipe was permanently repaired in a few days, it would be impossible for him to enter the vault without authorization and without there being a record of it. He had to move fast.

That same shift, Lt. Blalock reconnoitered the Babette Craven Art vault while conducting a…Water Watch he guessed was the proper term. When security patrols to visually check for signs of fire while the fire alarm system is out, it's called a Fire Watch. Why not Water Watch when they are checking for leaks? And Psycho Watch while keeping their eyes peeled for James Moll?

Blalock waltzed his way into the vault through the back way and once inside, he pulled blue latex gloves from a pants pocket, snapped them on, and then walked briskly to the ornate jewelry casket. He marveled at it for a few moments and then removed the 4G iPhone burner Whyte had provided. He took photos of the box on all sides, from different angles, turning the box as needed.

Norman grinned as he photographed the jewelry box.

[0000]

Blalock arranged another meeting at the "Whyte House" that night. He filled in Whyte on the new security measures and then told him, "For now, I can get into the vault on the pretense that I'm checking for leaks from that busted pipe, but I've got to work fast before they upgrade security and repair the water pipe early next week. SPO Thomas will be on leave on Monday and I've taken his evening shift, 1400 – 2200 hours. There's a performance of Othello that evening. They use haze as a special effect. Haze will set off the fire alarm and the fire suppression system in the theatre, just like smoke from a fire, so we have to turn off the fire alarm for each show and conduct Fire Watches during each performance to visually inspect the building for fire while the system is out. During a Fire Watch, I will check the art vault for leaks, as ordered, because I will also be the Water Watch Officer. I'll get the BlackBerry then."

Whyte smiled and said, "Excellent."

"Now," said Norman, "teach me how to work the…Chinese puzzle on the bottom of the box and then hand over the rings."

Mr. Whyte laid the jewelry box on its back and said, "Watch closely…"

[0000]

A Remark You Made by Weather Report emanated from the limo's premium sound system as they were driven back to Blalock's house.

While sipping Gin Martinis and smoking cigarettes like Bogie and Bacall, Kavitha said to Norman, "Monday is Halloween you know."

Norman shrugged. "So?"

"The realms of the living and the dead are closest on All Hallows' Eve," Kavitha offered. "The dead can more readily commune with the living. Aren't you worried about the Folgers?"

Norman shook his head and sighed. "Are you really superstitious or are you just trying to mess with my mind? Besides, why would the Folgers object to me helping to bring an end to the controversy over their beloved Shakespeare?"

Kavitha laughed insincerely and said, "I was just messing with your mind, that's all. I *know* you're afraid of them."

Norman smiled and replied, "Not as afraid as I am of you, Junior."

[0000]

That night, while Kavitha was asleep in his bed, Norman downloaded to his laptop the photos he'd taken of the jewelry casket and then continued his research on the Internet. Before he returned to bed, he had the answers he was looking for.

He had difficulty falling asleep.

[0000]

Norman spent the day of Saturday, October 29th, with Kavitha. They had brunch at *Kramerbooks Afterwords Café* located in Dupont Circle, visited the Smithsonian Museum of American History located on the National Mall between Constitution Avenue and 14th Street, NW, and in the afternoon, took his dog Bruno for a walk in Lincoln Park.

Lincoln Square aka Lincoln Park is an urban park located in the Capitol Hill neighborhood of Washington, D.C. Maintained by the National Park service, Lincoln Park is situated one mile directly east of the United States Capitol, and is bounded by 13th Street NE and SE on the east and 11th Street NE and SE on the west, East Capitol Street NE on the North, and East Capitol Street SE on the south.

Planned by Pierre Charles L'Enfant in 1791 to be the point from which all distances in North America would be measured, officially named Lincoln Square by Congress in 1867, it was the first site to bear the name of the martyred President.

It was originally used as a dump, and then as the site for Lincoln Hospital during the civil war. Walt Whitman visited the patients there.

On April 14, 1876, the eleventh anniversary of President Lincoln's assassination, a memorial statue depicting Lincoln in his characteristic frock coat, holding the Emancipation Proclamation before a kneeling black man, his arms extended to show his broken shackles, was unveiled in the park with more than 25,000 people in attendance. Frederick Douglass delivered the keynote address before President Ulysses S. Grant, his cabinet and members of Congress. He discussed both his approval and disapproval of the monument, observing that the monument perpetuated many stereotypes about blacks' ability and participation in antislavery activity.

The President Lincoln statue originally had faced west towards the U.S. Capitol until it was rotated east in 1974 in order to face the newly-erected monument to educator and activist Mary McLeod Bethune, across the park at the west end. Bankrolled by funds raised by the National Council of Negro Women, the organization Mrs. Bethune founded in 1935, the statue depicts an elderly Mrs. Bethune supporting herself with a cane given to her by President Roosevelt and handing a copy of her legacy to two young black children. The statue was unveiled before a crowd of 18,000 on Mrs. Bethune's 99th birthday anniversary, July 10, 1974.

Norman Blalock was giving Kavitha the low down on the park as they stood before the Emancipation Memorial when he noticed a short and rotund well-dressed Asian man accompanied by what obviously must be his chauffer/body guard waddling toward them. The chauffer, who appeared to be Slavic...or Nordic...or Aryan, was stuffed into his uniform and reminded Blalock of the Schwarzeneggeresque actor in the popular hilarious Planet Fitness commercial, who swigs from a gallon jug of Orange juice and repeats in a thick, Schwarzenegger-like accent, "I lift things up and put them down."

"You will allow my driver to search you," the Asian demanded. "Hans."

The Aryan Lifter took a step toward them, but stopped dead in his tracks when Bruno growled low and throaty and bared his big, white fangs. The hair on the magnificent canine's back stood up, his tail curled into a tight knot up on his back, and the beast strained against his leash, pulling in the direction of Hans and the Asian, like a police-trained K-9. Norman felt an instant twinge of pride. But then mused, *Pride goeth before destruction, and an haughty spirit before a fall...*

Blalock's hand shot to his side, to the holstered Glock .45 under his jacket. He barked, "Back the fuck up, Hans. You just going to walk up on a big ass dog like this? Just because your midget-ass boss says so? Really? Is that how you roll in Berlin? Well, you're in DC now, Nazi boy."

The Asian extended both hands. "It's for my own protection, Dr. Blalock…"

"Stay on my good side and you'll be safe, Frodo," Blalock assured him. "What's this all about?"

The Asian man, still with his hands outstretched, pleaded, "Kavitha…?"

Norman stared at Kavitha. She shrugged.

Kavitha and the fat man had a conversation in what Norman supposed was Japanese.

Satō

彼は、会議についての教えてくれなかったですか?

Kavitha

心に留めてことはありません。彼だけは、取引している!

"I arranged this meeting, Norm," she confessed. "This is Mr. Satō. He's got a better offer. Hear him out."

Norm lowered his gun-hand and said, "I'm listening."

"I am a competitor of Mr. Whyte," Satō explained. "The prize he is seeking is not in the Folger vault."

Norman frowned.

"There is a third jewelry casket," Mr. Satō continued. "The one with Shakespeare's BlackBerry, one which needs a third mourning ring to open the secret compartment, the one *I* own." Mr. Satō removed a ring from a pocket of his suit jacket and held it up. I have one ring, but I also need Mr. Whyte's two mourning rings to open my casket, the *right* casket. I'll pay you ten million for them, Dr. Blalock."

Kavitha looked at Norman. She smirked and nodded her lovely head, her long black hair bouncing.

Norman Blalock shook his head a couple of times and said, "Wait. What?"

Mr. Satō took a half-step closer. "I can assure you, Dr. Blalock, I am willing to do whatever it takes to enlist your cooperation, even up to and including guaranteeing the safety of your family in these dangerous times, your children, even your ex-wife…"

Norm got up on his hind legs and Mr. Satō took a full-step back.

"Are you threatening my family?" Norm asked. "That's not business, that's personal. So personal, in fact, the only thing you can get out of it is a cap in your ass."

Using two fingers, Norm peeled back the right side of his jacket to reveal the butt of his Glock .45.

"We can all die right here, tonight," he assured the fat man and his companion. "This park was the site of Lincoln Hospital during the Civil War; this place is a graveyard already. The dead don't mind company.

"Now, business or personal, which is it?"

"Business," Mr. Satō answered.

Norm let his jacket fall and stood up straight and tall. "Let's talk business, then," he said.

"I offer you ten million dollars for Mr. Whyte's mourning rings."

"How will payment be made?" Norman wanted to know.

"Wire transfer on delivery," Satō told him.

"Half down," said Norman.

""Done," Satō agreed.

Norman pulled out of his pocket the cell phone Mr. Whyte had provided him and handed it to Mr. Satō. "Punch in a number I can reach you 24/7."

"Twenty-four seven?" Mr. Satō inquired.

"Twenty-four hours a day, seven days a week," Norman explained.

Mr. Satō nodded. "Oh, I see, yes."

Satō encoded his phone number and handed the cell phone back to Norm. Norm assigned a name to the number and saved it in his Contacts. Now there were two in this ghost phone's directory.

"Let me sleep on your generous offer, Mr. Satō,"

Norm said. "I'll let you know my decision tomorrow morning."

Mr. Satō nodded. "I anxiously await your decision, Dr. Blalock. Dr. Netram, I will be in touch with you, as well. Good night."

Norman nodded.

Kavitha said, "Good night."

Mr. Satō and his bodyguard/driver Hans turned and went back the way they came.

Blalock stared at the Bond Girl and shook his head. He had only wanted a peaceful and relaxing walk in the park but instead had gotten blindsided and now was anxious and flabbergasted.

"How many languages do you speak?" Norman asked.

"Seven," Kavitha answered. "How about you?"

"Who the hell *are* you, anyway?"

"I told you," Kavitha said. "I'm a businesswoman."

"You're a criminal!" Norman countered.

"Business *is* crime," she rebutted. "Norm, you have the opportunity to more than triple your take for less effort. Don't blow it. You don't owe the Folger and you sure as hell don't owe Whyte. Stiff him and go for the better deal. He'd stiff us. Nothing personal, mind you, it's just business."

"Us?" he asked.

She smiled and cooed, "We're a team, Norm."

"Are we?" asked Blalock.

Kavitha opened her jacket to reveal a pistol in a shoulder holster.

"I've got your back, Norm."

"Is that a Walther PPK?" Norman marveled.

Kavitha nodded.

"Who the hell *are* you anyway?" Norm asked. "I don't even know you. Trust you?"

She laid an elegant hand softly on his chest and gave him a wet kiss. And then her dark, soul-piercing eyes met his.

"Of course," she said sincerely. "Trust me."

"Trust you," Norman snorted. He didn't trust her as far as he could throw her.

"Who else are you going to trust?" she purred.

Norman replied, "Honor among thieves, huh?"

Kavitha nodded. "Honor among thieves, yes. They say there is no honor among thieves, but there is." She stepped back, spat in her hand, and extended it to Norm. "Honor among thieves."

Norman spat in his own hand and shook her wet hand.

"Honor among thieves," he agreed. "So, what's the plan?"

Kavitha let go of his hand and took his arm.

Norm said, "Yeah, you think you're slick, but I feel you wiping our spit on my sleeve. Uh huh."

"This is what we'll do," she said.

Kavitha told Norm her plan as they and Bruno the Wonder Dog walked away from the Mary McLeod Bethune Memorial and out of the park.

"You'll use Rupert's rings to take a look in the jewelry box. If the BlackBerry is there, we'll hang on to it and you'll just tell him the box was empty. I know a man in Amsterdam who'll pay twenty million for the BlackBerry. And if it's empty, that's okay too. You'll still have the five hundred thousand deposit from Whyte. And we'll sell Whyte's morning rings to Satō for ten million and I'll give Rupert perfect replicas of his rings that I commissioned in Hong Kong. He won't know the difference. When you leave the vault…"

Norman frowned as he listened to Kavitha.

As she outlined her plan, he recalled something his old friend Homicide Detective John Mayfield had once told him:

The devil is always depicted as a hideous beast with horns and a tail, he's not. The devil is not repulsive, he's attractive. Evil must be inviting...seductive. The devil is a handsome man, a beautiful woman.

Norman did not doubt it now.

[0000]

Later that evening, sitting in his living room in his favorite overstuffed chair, *Holdin' Back the Years* performed by Jazz trumpeter Rick Braun quietly emanating from his vintage TEAC reel-to-reel, Norman watched Kavitha looking over his acquisitions as he smoked a cigarette and sipped cognac.

Kavitha took a drag from her Sobranie Black Russian, an elegant cigarette rolled in black paper with a gold colored filter, then exhaled blue smoke.

"You've got some really great pieces here, Norman. Antiques worthy of a museum."

"They'll end at the pawn shop, the Good Will, or in the city dump," he said.

"Why do you say, that Norman? Some of this stuff is...priceless."

"My heirs think this stuff is junk," he confided. Norman paused and then said, "Lately, I find myself wondering what's going to happen to all this stuff when I'm gone. My children aren't interested in any of it, or the house for that matter. My grandfather bought this place. He left it to my dad, who left it to me. I'll leave it to my son, but he doesn't want the house. He'll sell it. Like your boss said, it's worth around $1.9 million. More than likely, my son will just trash the contents of the house."

"That's a shame," she said. "Maybe you can turn it into a museum, like Cedar Hill."

"That's not likely," Norman snorted. "Frederick Douglass was an important man, he made history. I've done nothing; my home doesn't rate being preserved as a museum."

"You're about to do something very important, Norm. In time, who knows? Your home might rate being a museum after all."

"Time will tell," Norm said.

"Yes," Kavitha agreed. "Time will tell."

Kavitha picked up a framed photo off the mantel over the fireplace and walked over to him. "Is this your father?"

"Yeah," he said. "That's my father, that's me, and that's my brother, Nathan."

"You look like your father."

"Yeah," Norman agreed. "We wore the same size clothes and shoes. I'm glad. I really love his wardrobe of vintage clothes and shoes. They're classic."

"They suit you," she said. "No pun intended."

Norman took the photo from her and looked at it for a time. *Holdin' Back the Years* faded out and Earl Klugh performing *Face in the Wind* faded in.

Out of the blue, Norman said, "My older brother Nathan was pop's favorite. Nathan got killed in Iraq. Pops wore Nate's dog tags around his neck on the same chain as his own, the ones he got when he was fighting the VC in Vietnam. He wore them 'til the day he died."

Norman reached inside his shirt and pulled out four dog tags dangling from a chain.

"These dog tags. When my father got old and sick, I took care of him right up to the end, without any help from my two brothers and two sisters. I lived with him, here in the house where I grew up. I lived with him ever since my marriage crumbled in. He charged me rent though. Not half as much as it would have cost me to pay rent anywhere else. It made it possible for me to pay child support for the twins without having to live out of my car. Pops said, 'You can't stay here for free. A man has to pay his own way.'

"When he died, he left me everything, other than the

family business, which I urged him to leave to my son. The house and everything in it, the car, everything. Who the hell else was he going to leave it to? The best part was when the lawyer gave me an envelope marked in Pops' own hand, 'For Norman – Open upon my death.'

"Inside was the combination to his safe. I opened the safe and found a note informing me that all the money I'd ever paid Pops for rent was inside. In cash. Pops always made me pay my rent in cash. More than twenty years worth, over one hundred thousand dollars."

Blalock shook his head, set down his drink, and mashed out his cigarette in the ashtray on the coffee table. He stared at the floor.

"Imagine that," he said.

After a time, Kavitha took the photo from him and replaced it on the mantel.

"My kids don't care for me," Norman confessed. "They loved their granddad, I guess because my ex liked him and didn't bad mouth him like she bad mouthed me, not that I blame her.

"Even my father had one person he could count on when he was failing. I'm not so fortunate."

Kavitha walked over to him and mashed out her cigarette in the ashtray on the coffee table. She leaned over, and took his face in her hands. She looked him directly in the eye and said, "You can count on me, Norm. I promise."

She kissed him like she really meant it.

As if on cue, *Face in the Wind* faded out and George Howard performing *Just for Tonight* faded in as they embraced, like lovers.

When the truth is too painful, we choose to live a lie. Norman chose to live the lie for now.

[0000]

Norman, Shakespeare's BlackBerry in hand, found himself running through the book stacks on Beta Deck. The fire alarm was sounding and the Halon Fire Suppression System was warning him to exit the area before the Halon gas was released. "A fire has been detected. Halon gas will be released in the area in two minutes. Clear the area."

The faster Norman tried to run, the slower he moved.

"A fire has been detected. Halon gas will be released in one minute. Clear the area."

Norman was moving in the slow motion and the nearest exit seemed to be getting farther and farther away.

"Halon gas will be released in thirty seconds. Clear the area."

Norman was now moving in ultra slow motion.

He heard the electronic locks on the exit doors click. Halon gas filled the room.

Norman, struggling for air, slowly sank to the floor, coughing.

He woke with a start, but he didn't disturb Kavitha sleeping next to him. Relieved it had only been a dream; he breathed deeply, and stared at the ceiling.

It took quite some time before he went back to sleep.

[0000]

On the morning of Sunday, October 30th, Norman picked up his ghost cell phone off his dresser and called Satō. When the Japanese businessman answered, Norman told him, "I accept your offer, Mr. Satō. Deposit three and a half million dollars in the Cayman National Bank, Grand Cayman Island this morning. I'm texting you the account number now. You'll deposit the balance just before delivery of the mourning rings. I'll let you know when and where."

Norman disconnected the call, opened a text message file for Satō, punched in his Cayman bank account number, pressed send, and then put the ghost phone back on his dresser.

[0000]

That night, Norman had another nightmare. He found himself in the lobby of the Folger's Elizabethan Theatre, holding Shakespeare's BlackBerry, rushing for the door and stopped in his tracks when he saw the head of Brenda Putnam's marble statue of Puck turn and its eyes fix on him.

Blalock gasped and then broke and ran to the double oak and glass doors leading to the vestibule, to the double aluminum and glass outer doors and escape, but found he could not open them.

The marble statue of Puck stood, stepped down off its pedestal, and walked toward Lt. Blalock, its arms outstretched.

Norman tried to run back the way he had come, but Puck caught him, whirled him around, lifted him off his feet, pressed him high against the wall, and started choking him with its cold Alabama marble hands.

Strangling as the cold stone hands throttled him, feet dangling, Norman stared into the smirking Puck's cold stone eyes, struggling in vain to pry Puck's hands from his throat. Right behind Puck, the transparent specters of Mr. and Mrs. Folger appeared and looked on. They smiled.

Norman woke with a start and sat bolt up. Heart pounding and sweating profusely, he rubbed his neck and tried to catch his breath.

He looked at Kavitha sleeping next to him. Again, he hadn't disturbed her. *She sleeps like a log*, he thought.

Again, it took him quite awhile to go back to sleep.

[0000]

Norman rose late in the day, after Kavitha was long gone. He went to the bathroom and washed his face and then went to his dresser. He opened the top drawer and removed a kit containing his blood sugar testing supplies, a small pump bottle of antibacterial hand sanitizer, and a blood pressure monitor, and placed them on top of the dresser. He opened the blood glucose testing kit, installed a new needle in the lancet, installed a testing strip in the blood glucose monitor and then sanitized his hands. Norman pricked one of his perpetually sore fingertips with the lancet, squeezed the pricked finger between two other sore fingers to get a good drop of blood, and then applied the drop to the test strip. He waited. In a few seconds, he read the results: 350. Damn! Two hundred thirty over his target level.

He attached a BD Ultra-Fine Pen Needle to his Lantus SoloStar Insulin Pen, dialed in a 20 ml dose, removed the needles safety cap and set the SoloStar aside while he pinched an inch of belly fat and swabbed it with a BD Alcohol Swab. He then picked up the insulin pen, quickly injected himself, removed the needle, and swabbed the injection site again.

Not yet finished playing his own doctor, Blalock put on his left bicep the blood pressure monitor's cuff and checked his blood pressure: 160 over 95. Not so good, considering normal blood pressure is 120 over 80 and his target range was 130 over 90, but not so bad considering.

Blalock checked his Seiko. He wasn't due to take his hypertension medications, 150 MG of Avapro, Lisinopril/HCTZ 20/25, 300 MG of Metoprolol, and 10 MG of Metolazone, and his cholesterol medication, 20 MG of Crestor for more than two hours.

He popped an 81 MG tablet of aspirin prescribed to be taken once daily to help prevent a heart attack.

And now, he had to make himself look presentable. He removed the blood pressure monitor cuff, packed up his kit, and tossed it back into the top dresser drawer.

He took clean underwear from another drawer and headed for the bathroom.

Standing in front of the mirror, Norman splashed hot water on his chin and jaws, squirt some shaving cream in his hand, and lathered his face. He grabbed his fully charged Norelco, the one advertised at one point as James Bond 007's new shaver, and went to work cleaning off gray beard stubble.

Norman then gargled, brushed his teeth, and then turned on and climbed into the shower.

Afterward, he dried himself and dressed in his bedroom and then returned to the bathroom and took stock of himself in the mirror.

Instead of the vintage clothes his father left, the man in the mirror wore a tan Pierre Cardin shirt and a tie with earth tone designs and a matching handkerchief in the breast pocket of a taupe colored worsted wool suit from Men's Wearhouse. The CEO of the company boasts about their clothing stock in his TV ads, "You're gonna like the way you look. I guarantee it."

As far as Norman Blalock was concerned, the CEO wasn't lying. Blalock liked the way he looked in all of his Men's Wearhouse suits, particularly this one. The suit jacket hung well. It was too bad he couldn't dress like this at work instead of that uniform. But he needed to look great when he and Kavitha went out on the town to celebrate after work, after he'd changed out of his uniform and hung it back in his locker.

Norman patted on some aftershave, Pinaud's Clubman, the stuff they use in barbershops.

He looked down at his shoes, Stacy Adams Concorde

Rust. Clean and scuff-free, they had the glass-like shine he insisted upon.

Norman couldn't resist, so he topped off his outfit by putting on one of his father's fedora, a tan one to match his new suit, and tugging it to a snug fit. He appraised himself in the mirror. Perfect.

He checked his Seiko. Time to head in to work. His lunch was already packed; so all he had to do was grab it out of the kitchen refrigerator on his way out to the garage.

Tonight was the night.

Consciously mocking the Bob Fosse character Roy Scheider portrayed in the motion picture *All That Jazz*, the man in the mirror smiled, held out his hands shoulder-high, and said, "It's show time."

[0000]

Elizabethan Garden, Folger Shakespeare Library Washington, D.C.

HALLOWEEN

Lt. Blalock, clean-shaven, tall, dark, and trim, wearing a fresh uniform consisting of navy blue slacks riding just right on the tops of spit-shined combat boots, a heavily starched white shirt choked by a navy blue necktie, and a navy blue commando sweater bearing on each sleeve blue, yellow and white circular Folger Shakespeare Library Police shoulder patches embroidered with Shakespeare's family crest and a shiny gold metal badge and matching name tag on either side of its half-bust circumference, stood bathed in floodlight in the Elizabethan Garden. A smoldering Sobranie Black Russian dangling from his full lips, he was watched over by masks of Comedy and Tragedy on the windowless east side of the library as he admired the sculpture of Hamlet, one of the garden's eight Greg Wyatt sculptures evoking characters and themes of Shakespeare's plays. As the Bard put it, "This garden has a world of pleasure in't."

The Elizabethan Garden, which has a knot garden, where Saffron crocuses were currently blooming, flowerbeds, hedges, and two benches nestled snuggly between two Magnolia trees at both its north and south ends and is surrounded by a wrought-iron fence with an entrance gate that is padlocked after hours, was inspired by herbal references in Shakespeare's plays, but also features popular plants of his age, such as English Ivy and lavender. At its center is a memorial to former Folger Director O.B. Hardison, an armillary sphere that serves as both a sundial and a garden ornament.

The garden is a great place to calm oneself and to collect one's thoughts, Blalock had found. He often picked one of the sculptures here to study in order to take his mind off his troubles, whenever he was trying to work things out in his mind. This time, he was there to muster his nerve. He prayed that he could pull off this heist and ride off into the sunset with a beautiful babe...and live happily ever after. Perhaps. If by some miracle the deal was legit. But he did not believe in miracles, nor did he believe in anyone.

Norman believed that in everyone's life there is one defining moment that sets the tone for their lives from that point on, whether or not they realize it. That moment for him came early on. He was three or four years old at the time.

Like his father's grandfather on his mother's side of the family, Pops played a game with him. He'd stand Norman on top of his dresser, take several steps back, and then tell him to jump. He'd catch Norman, stand him on top of the dresser, and they'd do it again. And again. "Weeee!" Norman giggled each time he leaped.

One day, the last day, they'd played their game, he jumped over and over again, and Pops caught him over and over again. Until the last round. "Jump," Pops told him. And he did. "Weee!" And while Norman was in midair, to his dismay, Pops turned his back on him and walked out of his bedroom. Norman hit the hardwood floor like a sack of potatoes.

As Pops walked down the hallway, without looking back, he said, "Never trust anybody. Not even me."

He'd followed that golden rule his whole life, even though distrusting everyone had never once protected or benefitted him, because he had still made bad decisions in spite of his distrust. Perhaps the outcome would be to his benefit this time...

Trick-or-treaters garbed as little ghouls, princesses, and superheroes walked by the front of the Folger on their way up East Capitol Street, giggling and holding their parents hands and bags of treats, interrupted Norman's thoughts. He looked at his watch: 2057 hours. It was time to go to the vault.

Lt. Blalock dropped what was left of his black and gold cigarette, extinguished it under a boot heel, and then strode away from the Hamlet sculpture, through the open gateway, up the east steps flanked by two marble benches and through one of the double aluminum doors at Door 48, the theater entrance of the building, a mask of Tragedy rising from the stone above the entry. He proceeded through the second set of double doors made of oak and into the into the Elizabethan Theatre lobby, an Elizabethan style chandelier with electric "candles" overhead, double doors of the theater itself flanked by the original Brenda Putnam Alabama marble statue of Puck and the wooden Docent's Desk directly ahead, the Box Office and stairwell to the theater balcony to his left, and on his right the Great Hall. Standing post there at the entrance to the theater lobby was part-time SPO Ann Swann, the Prince George's County, Maryland high school principal, with a PhD in education.

"How's it going, Ann?" asked Blalock.

"Good, Norm," SPO Swann replied. "You?"

"Good," Blalock lied.

Production Manager/Technical Director Charles Flye bounded down the balcony stairwell two steps at a time, as usual. Blalock fist-bumped the jovial slender young man.

"How's it going, Norm?"

"Good," said Blalock. "You're always in a good mood, Charles. You must be the happiest man in the world."

"Yes," Charles agreed. "Yes, I am. I've got a great family, a great job, got my health. What more can anyone ask for?"

Norman nodded. "Nothing. Catch you later."

"Later," Charles said and then he bounded out Door 48.

Lt. Blalock turned and proceeded through the Great Hall with its 30-foot plaster strapwork ceiling adorned here and there with Shakespeare's coat of arms, Appalachian white oak paneling, and ornamental floor tiles, where the current exhibition was the extremely popular *Manifold Greatness: The Life and Afterlife of the King James Bible*. With so many bibles about, it was a perfect place to pray, so he did. Under his breath, Norman said, "Please, God, don't let me get caught."

SPO Cary was on the desk at Central.

"Hey, Luther," Blalock greeted SPO Cary, who nodded at him.

"How's it going, Norm?"

"Just fine," Blalock replied. "I'm going to do another Fire Watch. I'll call it in."

"Good," said Luther. "Don't forget to check the art vault for leaks."

"Sure thing," Blalock said.

Norman casually said hello to Kavitha Netram, his co-conspirator, who was sitting at the Gift Shop Desk, and she casually said hi. He then ran up the three steps leading to an Authorized Personnel Only zone of the Folger and proceeded down the hall to the elevator on his left. He pressed the call button and the doors opened immediately. He walked into the elevator and pressed 3. If the elevator records were pulled, they would confirm that someone, that *he*, had used the elevator to go to the top floor at that time. Also, Luther would assume he had, as usual, started his Fire Watch on the top floor of the west wing.

On the third floor, he got off, turned right, and ran down the stairs to the basement.

Stealthily, making sure not to make the wooden stairs creak, he made his way up the stairs as quickly as possible while being silent. On the first floor, he took a peek to make sure no one was watching, turned left and tiptoed to the door to of the Registrar's Office. Quietly, he opened the door, entered, and silently closed the door behind him.

Blalock proceeded through a set of double wood and glass doors, through the Gail Paster Reading Room, through the half-door next to the Librarian's Desk, and through a wooden door leading to a stairwell. Keys in hand, he ran down three flights of carpeted stairs to Gamma Deck, unlocked a metal door, and slowly opened it. He looked around the space on the other side of the door to make sure that he was alone and then entered, closing the door after him. He ran past the biometric security entrance to the vault on his left over to a wooden door directly ahead of him, unlocked it, and went through. He ran down the hallway to another wooden door, unlocked it, and went through. He ran down another hallway to a metal door on his left, but then stopped dead in his tracks when he heard the keys jingling on the Sam Browne belt of a member of the Armed Response Team on a random roving patrol somewhere in the books stacks of the immense Gamma Deck. And then he heard a voice communication between Central and Adam-13 crackle from the rover's radio, closer still. The rover was headed his way. He didn't want anyone to be able to say later that they had seen him anywhere near this area or what time they had seen him there, so Blalock quickly tiptoe-ran to the door leading to a storage/elevator service area, opened the door, and closed it quietly behind him.

Gasping for air, he struggled to control his rapid breathing. What was that sound? Was the K-9 officer coming Blalock's way?

After what seemed like an eternity, he cracked the door and listened for awhile. He heard nothing.

Lt. Blalock exited the room, sprinted to a metal door on his right, unlocked it, and went through into another long hallway. On his left, he unlocked another metal door and went through, to Door 44. He unlocked Door 44 and walked into a small room and then unlocked and walked through another metal door on the other side of that room. At that point, he was behind the locked Mosler vault door on the front side of Gamma Deck; he had entered the vault area via the back way for the use of authorized personnel in case of an emergency.

Blalock moved past the Halon Closet, past the elevator to the Omega Deck, unlocked the metal door to the Babette Craven Art Vault, and walked through the door. He was in.

Perspiring and breathing heavily, his back against the door, he stood in the dark for a few moments to catch his breath and then flicked the light switch. He pulled blue latex gloves from a pants pocket, snapped them on, and then pushed off the door and walked briskly to the ornate jewelry casket. He marveled at it for a few moments and then removed and set aside two red velvet covered jewelry trays one after the other, and tilted the box over onto its back. He took the two mourning rings from a pants pocket, laid them on the shelf next to the jewelry box, and then started moving the Chinese puzzle pieces on the bottom of the jewelry box.

[0000]

Whyte was sitting in the back of his black Lincoln limo when his cell phone rang. The caller ID told him it was Blalock. He answered it, speaking into his Bluetooth. "Yes?"

"Shakespeare's BlackBerry, huh?" Blalock said. "You *do* think I'm a fool. This writing table didn't belong to Shakespeare."

"Dr. Blalock," said Whyte, "Does it really matter whose BlackBerry it is? Really? Three million dollars, Doctor. Give me the BlackBerry and it's yours."

"Does it matter if Shakespeare was Shakespeare?" Blalock countered.

"Of course," Whyte yelled. "Of course it matters!"

Blalock said, "You don't want to prove Shakespeare was Shakespeare, you want to prove that he *wasn't*. I knew that a few days after you told me that bullshit story. Condell and Heminge had no reason to hide Shakespeare's BlackBerry, no reason to keep it a secret. So I researched the family crests on the jewelry box, the three other than Shakespeare's, to look for clues to what you were really after."

Rupert Whyte swallowed hard.

"I was sure that two of the three must be Condell's and Heminge's," Blalock continued, "but I was wrong. I discovered that the other family crests belonged to Ben Jonson, the Herbert Brothers, and Edward de Vere. It was then I speculated that this had possibly been a conspiracy to conceal the author's identity until a later date, sometime in the 17th Century perhaps. I suspect something went wrong and the secret got mislaid until you and your Oxfordian friends got wind of it.

"Even if I hadn't suspected your deception and had not done some sleuthing, knowing how to read Old English would have given you away. Betsy Walsh taught me how years ago and I've been practicing. Practice makes perfect."

"Then you have the proof?" Whyte asked. "The BlackBerry contains the signed confession of Heminges and

Condell regarding the First Folio and the identity of the true author of the collected works, in their own hand?"

"The works speak for themselves," Blalock argued.

"Who cares who wrote them?"

"The world must know the truth!" Whyte screamed. "The Shakespeare hoax is a literary deception that has gone on for far too long and must finally be exposed. As a consequence of this revelation, speculations about the sources and meanings of the canon of work falsely attributed to the man from Stratford-upon-Avon will become a sick joke and analyses of plays and poems will have to be rewritten, the history of Elizabethan drama and poetry will have to be drastically revised. This revelation will rock the very foundation of English Literature and your precious library's mission to advance knowledge and the arts will halt until it is renamed the Folger de Vere Library!"

"Okay," Blalock acquiesced. "Whatever. Listen, I don't have a dog in this fight. I don't give a shit who the author was. But my price for the BlackBerry is now five million. Because you mistook me for a fool. You've got five minutes to deposit the money or I'll wipe every page clean."

"No!" Whyte yelled. "You wouldn't."

"Try me," said Blalock.

"Five million, yes," Whyte agreed.

"When I see the money has been deposited, the BlackBerry's yours," Blalock said.

"I'm transferring the funds now," said Whyte. "And don't try to cross me, Dr. Blalock. I always hedge my bets."

"That can only mean you have someone else besides Kavitha on the inside," Norman said. Blalock disconnected the phone call. "Another guard," he said under his breath.

Whyte looked at his cell phone, speed-dialed a number, and then opened his laptop and started typing on its keyboard. "Yes," he said. "He's got it and he's threatened to destroy it. Take it from him. Check your tracker! My readings indicate…he's on the roof!"

Blalock speed-dialed Satō. When the Japanese businessman answered, he said. "Deposit the balance now." "What?" Satō asked. "But, I've already deposited the balance. Ms. Netram contacted me a little while ago and gave me another account number. What is going on?" "Just a miscommunication," Blalock lied. "We'll be in touch."

Blalock discontinued the phone call and hissed, "Dirty bitch!"

He pulled from his pants pocket a second burner, the same model as his personal cell phone, which he'd purchased the day before while he was running errands, and worked the Smartphone's keys; he had to conduct his banking transactions swiftly.

Afterward, Blalock made his way down from the roof, to the third floor. He turned right and hurried down the hall past the Werner Gundersheimer Conservation Laboratory on his left, and then ducked into Mechanical Room #7 located at the opposite end of the hall from the "ART DEPT." He ran up the stairs to Catwalk #1 and ran toward the door at the other end.

"Where are you going, lieutenant?"

Lt. Blalock stopped in his tracks and turned to find muscle-bound, platinum blonde Armed Response Team Sgt. Lou Carew standing at the top of the stairs the lieutenant had just used to get to the catwalk.

Sgt. Carew smiled and held out his iPhone. "You're Lojacked."

"So it's you, huh?" Lt. Blalock asked. "When did she get to you?"

Sgt. Carew chuckled and walked toward Lt. Blalock. "Boy, have you got the wrong guy. Rupert is my friend."

Lt. Blalock shook his head. "It's always you big, muscle-bound he-men, isn't it?"

"Cut the crap, old man. Give it to me."

"I don't have it," said Blalock, backing away. "The

jewelry box was empty…"

"Bullshit!" Sgt. Carew yelled. "Give it to me and you won't get hurt."

"Why don't you shoot me and take it?"

"I don't need a gun to take you out," Sgt. Carew assured him.

"Shoot me or beat me to death, it doesn't make much difference," Lt. Blalock said. "You can't get away with it so long as I'm alive."

"Then you'll have to die," Sgt. Carew said flatly.

Sgt. Carew ran toward Lt. Blalock.

As soon as Carew was within striking distance, Blalock punched him in his windpipe. The behemoth stopped in his tracks, clutching his throat with both hands, gasping for air.

"I guess Rupert didn't tell you I have a black belt in Karate," said Blalock. "Maybe he didn't know."

Blalock closed the distance between him and the door at the other end of Catwalk #1. He opened the door and then turned around to climb down the ladder at that end, only to find the still gasping Sgt. Carew had closed the distance as well, and was reaching for Norman. Carew grabbed his sweater and when he jerked free, Blalock lost his footing and fell to the floor below, just outside of Mechanical Room #5. He heard bones in his right ankle snap and instantly felt white hot pain.

As he grimaced, Lt. Blalock looked up and saw the face of the now unconscious Sgt. Carew hanging over the doorframe at the top of the ladder. Blalock stood and, wincing all the way, opened the door to Mechanical Room #5 and went in. He quickly found a toolbox, opened it, and found duct tape inside. With alacrity, he wrapped duct tape around and around his broken ankle to give it some support and then cut his makeshift bandage free from the roll with a box cutter he also found in the toolbox and then cut two strips about 8 inches in length and attached them to the back of his hand to use later...

Blalock tossed the box cutter back into toolbox the removed the back from the "ghost phone" Whyte had supplied him. He removed the iPhone's battery, took out its SIM card, and crushed it under the boot heel of his good foot. Afterward, he put Whyte's iPhone back together, picked up the shattered SIM card and tossed it into a huge trash can full of industrial rubbish. Wincing with every hop-step, he then exited Mechanical Room #5, turned left, and walked past the Elizabethan Theatre's control booth and took the steps down from the third floor of the theatre to backstage, where he wiped all of his fingerprints off all sides of the ghost phone using the front of his sweater and then tossed the Whyte's burner into a box of props.

Lt. Blalock peeked from backstage to make sure the theatre was empty. It was; it was intermission and all the patrons were out in the Great Hall, where concessions were on sale...

Norman keyed his radio and said, "Adam-3 to Central."

"Go ahead for Central," SPO Luther Cary's voice came over the radio.

"Fire and Water Watches complete," said Blalock. "All clear in the art vault and east and west wings secure."

"10-4," SPO Cary said. "At 2117 hours."

Blalock exited the Elizabethan Theatre and hobbled into the theatre lobby.

"What's wrong with your leg?" SPO Swann asked.

"Oh, I just sprained my ankle," Lt. Blalock lied. "Tripped coming down the stairs."

"You look terrible," said Swann. "You're sweating. You should go to the infirmary."

"I'm on my way now," Blalock said.

Norman walked into the Great Hall and made his way through the crowd of theater goers who were buying and consuming concessions during the intermission for Othello and then entered the Gail Paster Reading Room via the unlocked east double metal and glass door, the one he'd opened earlier to accommodate a wheelchair-bound patron and allow him access to the theater.

Sgt. Lou Carew made his way through the crowd, following him...

[0000]

Blalock, perspiring and breathing heavily, had paused and looked at the portraits of Henry Clay and Emily Folger painted by renowned artist Frank O. Salisbury in 1927, located in the Gail Paster Reading Room, under a replica of William Shakespeare's tomb and straddling the back wall with the columbarium niche containing the Folgers' urns concealed behind a brass plaque with an etched crucifix above the inscription:

TO THE GLORY OF
WILLIAM SHAKESPEARE
AND THE GREATER GLORY
OF GOD

HENRY CLAY FOLGER
JUNE 18 1857
JUNE 11 1930

EMILY CLARA JORDAN FOLGER
MAY 15 1858
FEBRUARY 21 1936

Suddenly, his left arm went numb and he felt excruciating pain in his chest, as though his heart were being gripped in a vise. He took his radio from his Sam Browne belt, keyed it, but could not speak. He dropped his radio and collapsed to the carpeted floor.

Not now, Norman thought...

[0000]

Kavitha Netram was sitting in the Gift Shop, checking her watch, when there was the sound of breaking glass coming from the hallway of the Authorized Personnel Only section nearby.

"What the...," SPO Luther Cary exclaimed.

Just then, the message came over the radio: "Adam-69 to Central, have someone respond to the Old Reading Room with the AED ASAP and call an ambulance. Blalock is down and I'm starting CPR."

"Central copy," SPO Cary spoke into the radio. "Any available Adam unit to assist."

"Adam-21 copy!" a voice came over the radio.

SPO Cary picked up the receiver on the desk phone and dialed 911.

Kavitha declared, "I'm CPR trained."

Her knee-high black leather high-heel boots clicking like cat claws on the slate floor, she ran to the door of the Registrar's Office and noticed broken glass underfoot and observed an octagonal section of glass cleanly cut within the borders of one of the octagon designs on the glass door was missing. It was curious, but she had no time to ponder it. Kavitha opened the door and ran through the office, through the double wood and glass doors and into the Gail Paster Reading Room.

Kavitha found a big and beefy platinum blonde guard wearing snug-fitting navy blue BDU's kneeling beside Norman.

"Get the AED," she told the muscle-bound guard. "I'm CPR trained."

Lou Carew aka Adam-69 stood and ran from the room, a Heckler & Koch MP5 submachine gun dangling from a strap slung over his right shoulder.

Kavitha ran to Norman where he lay near the back wall, in close proximity to the Folgers' urns entombed in a columbarium niche behind a memorial plaque straddled by portraits of Henry Clay and Emily. Before she started CPR, Kavitha quickly checked Blalock's shirt and pants pockets, but did not find the BlackBerry, only his cell phone, the mourning rings, and his personal keys in his pants pockets. She left the cell phone where it was, but hid the rings in her bra and put Norman's keys inside her left boot. Then she went to work on him.

When Adam-69 returned with the Automated External Defibrillator (AED), SPO Donnell Curtis on his heels, she continued CPR until Adam-69 was ready to use the AED. Adam-69 removed the AED from its case and turned it on. The AED spoke: *"Begin by removing all clothing from the patient's chest..."*

SPO Curtis told Kavitha to back away and then quickly pulled Blalock's sweater over his head and off his arms and tossed it. He then ripped open Blalock's shirt, sending buttons flying in all directions, and used scissors to cut Blalock's tee shirt up the middle. Adam-69 applied the electrodes to Blalock's chest, making certain that the adhesive backed pads were securely affixed.

AED: *"Stand clear. No one should touch the patient. Analyzing heart rhythm. Shock advised..."*

"Clear!" Adam-69 yelled.

Kavitha was dismayed, yet her mind was reeling. She stared at the portraits of the Folgers on the back wall as she considered what she was going to tell Mr. Whyte about this fiasco.

The writing table was not on Blalock, but Whyte would believe there were only two possibilities: either Blalock had hidden the writing table somewhere in the building or she had stolen it from Blalock as he lay dying on the floor of the Gail Paster Reading Room in order to broker her own deal for its sale to one of his competitors behind his back. Therefore, she would forever be under his scrutiny.

Maybe in the end Norman had not trusted them...*her*, after all; maybe he'd decided not to give the artifact to them until he could be sure of his safety and had in fact hidden it somewhere. But she didn't believe so. She was certain that she had had Norman wrapped around her little finger, that he had had no idea that part of her contract was to kill him once Shakespeare's BlackBerry was in hand...at which time Whyte, with the help of the president of the Swiss bank he'd referred Norman to, would withdraw the funds from Norm's account and redeposit the money in his own. S.O.P. And cracking that Cracker Jack box of an antique floor safe of Norman's in his basement, which she was certain Norman didn't know she knew about, and retrieving the negotiable bearer bonds and cash would have been a snap for her.

Regardless, she would never reveal to Whyte that she felt guilty about setting Norman up; nor that she believed the Folgers themselves somehow had orchestrated Blalock's demise from beyond the grave and had taken the writing table. Furthermore, she would never divulge that she was certain the Folger Shakespeare Library had the best security anywhere and any attempt to defile this institution would prove futile.

Intuition informed her that security personnel there are not the only ones guarding Shakespeare.

At first, she couldn't quite put her finger on the feeling that was quickly overcoming her and then she was struck by the starting revelation that it was remorse that she was feeling. There's a first time for everything.

She was also astonished to learn that she was going to miss him. At the very moment she realized this, Norman stirred and started coughing and Kavitha's heart leapt.

AED: "*Shock not recommended...*"

Lou Carew jumped to his feet. "I'm going to go check

on that ambulance."

SPO Carew ran from the Gail Paster Reading Room, but stopped in the Registrar's Office. He pulled out his cell phone and speed-dialed a number. He put the phone to his ear, waited a few moments and then said, "He didn't have it on him."

"You're kidding, Lou," Rupert Whyte said on the other end. "You got to him first, didn't you?"

"Yes," SPO Carew said. "It wasn't on him. He must have hid it. He had a heart attack, but he's coming around. We'll make him tell us where it is."

Whyte disconnected the phone call.

"Rupert?" Carew said. "Rupert?"

SPO Carew put away his cell phone and ran to the west lobby. Just as he arrived, recently fired Officer James Moll, armed with a Colt .45 semiautomatic pistol and wearing camouflage BDUs, war paint, and his new hairdo, cornrows flowing down his back, the seashells on the tips of each extension clacking together as they swished from one shoulder to the other, entered through Door 49. Carew instantly raised and aimed his MP5 submachine gun. SPO Luther Cary ducked and reached for one of the hidden pistols in the guard's desk just as SPO Carew and James Moll opened fire on each other.

SPO Carew fired bullets into James Moll that struck from his belly button to his forehead and Moll's one shot struck Carew square in the forehead. Both simultaneously dropped to the slate floor like sacks of potatoes.

SPO Cary, gun in hand, went to Moll and kicked away his weapon from his dead hand. He then got on the desk phone and once again dialed 9-1-1.

[0000]

Washington Hospital Center
Washington, D.C.

November 2nd, 11:43 a.m.

When Blalock came to, he was lying in bed…in a hospital room. Sensors to monitor his vital signs were taped to him…and an IV drip was going…and his right leg was in a cast, elevated above the bed in a sling. And then it came to him. He remembered how he'd ended up there and then began to wonder how long he'd been there.

A young Asian nurse entered the room shortly after he came around.

"Well, well," the nurse said, "look who's finally awake. What's your name?"

Blalock squinted at her and in a hoarse voice replied, "Norman. Blalock."

"Good," said the nurse. "You haven't had a stroke since last we talked. What's my name?"

"Annie. Yu," Blalock told her.

Nurse Yu nodded. "That's right." She picked up off a side table a white Styrofoam cup with a lid and a straw and put the straw between his lips. "Take a sip." She returned the cup to the table. "I'm going to get your doctor. I'll be right back."

The nurse left the room and returned shortly with a doctor who looked Middle-Eastern. He said his name was Dr. Hussein and described the angioplasty procedure he'd performed on him, Norman's heart ailment, and the statistics for recovery and for extending life following a heart attack with proper care.

Dr. Hussein finished his spiel by saying, "You're a very lucky man, Mr. Blalock. You've been given a second chance. Don't waste it."

"I'll do my best, Doc," Norman pledged. "Thank you."

Dr. Hussein nodded. "My pleasure, sir."

Kavitha Netram entered the room as Nurse Yu and Dr. Hussein were walking out. The doctor ogled her as best he could in the brief moment he had. He wished he had waited a few seconds before committing to leaving so he could have lingered and looked the beauty over properly. Indeed, she was worthy of a closer look.

Wearing a tight, form-fitting short black dress with spaghetti straps, black pumps, and those black silk stockings with the seams up the back she knew he liked, a black leather handbag thrown over one bare, golden shoulder, raven hair tossed over the other, she was a sight for sore eyes. She struck a pose and smirked, "You don't look bad for a dead man."

She sashayed over to the bed and hopped onto it. Blalock bounced on the bed. His leg in the sling shook and swung side to side and he winced.

Kavitha shrugged and smiled. "Sorry."

Blalock frowned at her.

"So," she said, "how do you feel?"

Blalock said, "Pretty good for a dead man."

Kavitha snickered and nodded. "You're lucky to be alive. You'd be dead if the Folgers had wanted it that way..."

Norman raised a hand and said, "Please."

"It's true you know. I'll tell you all about it one day."

"Okay, Junior."

"So, tell me, what's it like on the other side?"

"It's a secret," Norman said. "If I tell you, I'd have to kill you."

Kavitha giggled.

Norman looked at her for a time and then asked, "Where's your boss?"

"He's around," she said. "He has to close this deal before he goes anywhere."

"You here to close it for him, Junior?"

She shook her head. "He closes his own deals. I came

to see you on my own."

As if on cue, Mr. Whyte entered the room. Speak of the devil and he shall appear.

Ever dapper, cane in hand, Rupert Whyte sauntered over to the bed.

"Well, how are you feeling today, Dr. Blalock?"

"Fine for a dead man," Blalock answered.

Whyte chuckled. "Yes. Well. Are you feeling well enough to discuss business?"

Blalock nodded. "Of course."

"Where is the BlackBerry?" Whyte asked.

Norman shrugged. "I don't know."

Whyte took a deep breath and then said, "You have five million dollars of our...of my money and that's the best you can come up with...?"

"I don't even know if it was in the box," Norman argued. "I never saw it..."

"Please, Dr. Blalock!" Whyte yelled.

"I couldn't open it!" Blalock yelled. "When I removed the false bottom, there were cutouts for *three* mourning rings!"

Mr. Whyte was taken aback, was visibly shaken. "Three?"

"Yes," Blalock assured him. "Now, I don't know if the jewelry casket in the Folger vault is just another decoy or the real McCoy. All I know is there's a third mourning ring somewhere out there, and probably a third duplicate jewelry box identical to yours. Whatever the case may be, it's no longer possible to get at it in the Folger vault to find out, not now with the new security protocols in place. Besides, I'm retiring."

"A third ring," Whyte muttered. "Another decoy?"

After a time, Whyte composed himself and said, "There is still the matter of the five million. You transferred it from the numbered Swiss bank account in the same minute it was deposited..."

"Yeah," Blalock said, "and prevented you from withdrawing the money five minutes after you deposited it. I figured I'd better hang on to it for awhile. To renegotiate my fee."

"Tell me," Whyte asked, "Why did you asked for more money when you had nothing to sell?"

Norman smirked. "I figured a man like you would cover his bets and have someone else on the inside other than me and his girl."

Before he continued, Norman noted that Kavitha looked genuinely surprised by the revelation that Whyte had had another inside man.

Blalock looked Whyte directly in the eye and said, "I needed to buy some time to make it out of the building alive..."

"Just barely, it would seem," Whyte interjected. "What do you want?"

"One million," said Blalock. "An additional five hundred thousand dollars. For dying." He glanced at his IV and the electrode wires flowing from him and his elevated leg in a cast and added, "And for pain and suffering. And for having your boyfriend Carew try to kill me."

Whyte considered the price and agreed. "Very well. One million."

"Write down your account number and hand me your iPhone," Blalock said.

Whyte complied, using the back of a business card, and then handed the card and his iPhone to Blalock.

Norman typed on the iPhone's keypad and after a couple of minutes, handed back the card and the cell phone to Whyte. The Brit looked at the screen and was satisfied that four and a half million dollars had been deposited in his account. He then put away his cell phone and tucked the card into his shirt pocket.

Mr. Whyte twirled the cane. "I have no use for this. I still haven't acquired my Holy Grail, but I see no reason you shouldn't acquire yours."

Whyte handed Blalock the cane and said, "For services rendered."

Norman examined the cane and then whispered, "Frederick Douglass's walking stick."

He marveled at the cane with a white handle made of whalebone or ivory or something else exotic and expensive. Norman gripped the handle in one hand and the wooden cane in the other, pulled them slowly apart and revealed a sword. He smiled. He waved the rapier slowly in the air a few times and then sheathed it.

"Care to accompany me, my dear?" Whyte asked Kavitha. "I've got another job in Hamburg, something to pass the time while the search for the BlackBerry continues."

"No thanks, Rupert," she said. "I'll sit this one out."

"As you wish," Whyte said. "Until next time, Dr. Netram, Dr. Blalock."

Mr. Whyte exited the room.

"That was some bullshit," said Kavitha. "But that's okay, I like your style."

"What about the mourning rings?" Norman asked. "Did you give Satō the real ones and pass the fake ones to Whyte?"

"Of course, I switched the rings. That's why we don't have to worry about Rupert anymore. He's failed his boss Mr. Johnson too many times. And Rupert didn't know the difference between the real mourning rings and the replicas I gave him, but Mr. Johnson surely will. He'll believe Rupert ripped him off. And Johnson won't be happy Whyte gave you one million plus of his money for absolutely nothing in return. Oh, yeah, Rupert Whyte's days are numbered. Trust me."

Norman didn't trust her as far as he could throw her.

"That's good to know," he said.

"I had no idea he had someone else working inside," she said. "But we don't have to worry about his butt boy

Carew either. James Moll took care of him..."

"I know," said Norman. "I saw the bodies when the paramedics wheeled me out."

Kavitha nodded. "So, that's that."

Norman said, "I also know you clipped the 2.5 mil Satō owed me..."

"Satō owed *us*," Kavitha corrected him. "Yes, I took it. I deposited our money in a separate account for safekeeping..."

"*Our* money, huh?"

Kavitha slowly nodded as her soul-piercing dark eyes looked deep inside him. She said, "Yes, *our* money. We're a team."

"We're a team?" Norman asked.

Kavitha nodded slowly.

"You know," she said, "this could be the beginning of a beautiful friendship."

Norman smiled broadly.

"Oh," she said, "I picked up our Jag from Puck Circle. I've been thinking we should change the personalized tags to SPLENDA. Huh? What do you think?"

"How..."

"I lifted your keys," she said. "Well, you were dead, you didn't need them anymore."

"Tisk-tisk," said Norman. "Stealing from the dead."

"Oh," said Kavitha, "I've straightened up the house and I've been feeding Bruno and walking him. He ran out of *Blue Buffalo*, so I bought a new bag, the Lamb and Wild Rice blend. He *loooves* it!"

Norman smirked. "Okay. Thanks."

She took the cane from him and laid it on the bed next to him. "I'll take this home for safekeeping. I'll bring it back when they release you."

"Okay," said Norman.

Kavitha got up, grabbed the bed's control pad and elevated the back of his bed to position him upright, and then positioned his tray in front of him. She sat back down on the bed, grabbed her handbag, fished out an electronic pad, and placed it on the tray between them. "Fancy a game of chess?"

"Sure," said Norman.

"I'm black," she announced.

"No," he disagreed, "*I'm* black."

Kavitha sucked her teeth and turned the electronic chessboard around so black was in front of Norman.

"You know, we should have played this game a long time ago," she said.

Norman looked her straight in the eye and said, "We've been playing this game since we met, Junior."

Kavitha smiled and nodded. She then looked at the chessboard and pondered her first move.

Norman said, "Hey, you haven't broken into my safe, have you?"

Kavitha sucked her teeth. "Of course not. Stealing from you would be stealing from myself. You know, I think it's time I retire too; crime has paid well enough. Oh, I know, let's open an antique store in Georgetown. We'll call it, *Things Remembered*. Oh, and we'll play Jazz in the store during business hours. We'll be partners, fifty/fifty."

Norman smiled. He didn't know what her angle was, but he didn't feel like trying to figure it out just then. Instead, he chose to live the lie for the time being. He decided to relax and enjoy the ride while it lasted. He shrugged and said, "Whatever works."

Blalock watched Kavitha, thinking as he marveled at her extraordinary physical beauty and tried to reconcile it with what, by his estimation, must be a rotten core.

O brave new world, that has such people in't.

Finally, Kavitha made her first move, King's Pawn D to D4. Norman suspected her next move would be King's Pawn E to E3. He mirrored her opening move.

"Before we get the business started," she continued, "We need a vacation in paradise. Someplace warm and tropical, so I can work on my tan. The weather in England is bloody awful and I've been stuck here in this near-winter climate when I could have been stretched out on the beach somewhere. Even Malibu or Palm Beach would do right now. They don't compare to the white sand beaches of Europe or Aruba, mind you, but they would suffice right now. And soon. Just look at my color..."

Norman started to interrupt her and quip that to look his best on the beach; he'd have to wear a three-piece suit. Instead, he let his Bacall prattle on while he became lost in thought.

Satō would be pissed when he discovered that his jewelry box was empty. He might even eventually put two and two together and suspect the truth and come looking for him...for the both of them. But they would just have cross that bridge when they came to it.

Norman replayed in his mind what had transpired between the time Carew made him fall and break his ankle and when he'd entered the Gail Paster Reading Room through one of the glass and metal double-doors off of the Great Hall: Norman had crept into the Elizabethan Theatre during intermission and hid the writing table.

Should it become necessary for him to retrieve the writing table, he had hidden it where it was readily accessible to him and yet would never be noticed by anyone, not even members of the cleaning crew, and secured it there with two strips of duct tape...

Norman Blalock had been guarding Shakespeare for twenty-five years and he saw no reason to stop now.

THE END

Shakespeare Sonnet 76

Why is my verse so barren of new pride,
So far from variation or quick change?
Why with the time do I not glance aside
To new-found methods and to compounds strange?
Why write I still all one, ever the same,
And keep invention in a noted weed,
That every word doth almost tell my name,
Showing their birth and where they did proceed?
O, know, sweet love, I always write of you,
And you and love are still my argument;
So all my best is dressing old words new,
Spending again what is already spent:
For as the sun is daily new and old,
So is my love still telling what is told.

"The novella is one of the richest and most rewarding of literary forms...it allows for more extended development of theme and character than does the short story, without making the elaborate structural demands of the full-length book. Thus it provides an intense, detailed exploration of its subject, providing to some degree both the concentrated focus of the short story and the broad scope of the novel."

- Robert Silverberg

A Few Notable English Language Novellas

Charles Dickens' **A Christmas Carol**

Robert Louis Stevenson's **The Strange Case of Dr. Jekyll and Mr. Hyde**

H.G. Wells' **The Time Machine**

John Steinbeck's **Of Mice and Men**

Ernest Hemingway's **The Old Man and the Sea**

Herman Melville's **Billy Budd, Sailor**

John W. Campbell's **Who Goes There?**

Jack London's **The Call of the Wild**

Joseph Conrad's **Heart of Darkness**

George Orwell's **Animal Farm**

Anthony Burgess' **A Clockwork Orange**

Truman Capote's **Breakfast at Tiffany's**

Stephen King's **Rita Hayworth and the Shawshank Redemption**

ꝗꝓ Ram Press

PRAISE FOR QUINTIN PETERSON'S A Dark Place

"Quintin Peterson, a retired DC police officer and natural born writer, pens crime fiction that is earned and alive."

– George Pelecanos, author of **WHAT IT WAS** and **THE CUT**

"Quintin Peterson writes with authenticity and honesty won from years of being a street cop, and in his chilling A Dark Place, he takes readers past the boring CSI or 'profiling' of a serial killer to show us the heart and soul of the badges who bring such monsters to justice."

– James Grady, author of **SIX DAYS OF THE CONDOR DOGS** and **MAD DOGS**

"Quintin Peterson takes his readers into the dark places that only cops are compelled to enter. Then he shows them how such terrible access darkens the souls of those who enter too often. This dark, and well detailed, story is so real and so believable that it becomes a trip you won't soon forget."

– Retired NYPD Lt. Ed Dee, author of **THE CON MAN'S DAUGHTER** and **LITTLE BOY BLUE**

"You want to know how it's done? Read Quintin Peterson's A Dark Place. Of all the crime writers out there, he's the one wearing the badge. He writes with a sure hand and is certain to please. Sit back and get chilled...."

– Ridley Pearson, author of **THE BODY OF DAVID HAYES** and **THE RISK AGENT**

"A Dark Place is a chilling, expertly crafted thriller."

– Jim Patton, author of **THE SHAKE** and **DYING FOR DANA**

 **Ram Press**

Norman Blalock will return in THE VOYNICH GAMBIT
The most mysterious book in the world is up for grabs.

Listening to the next song on her iPod playlist as she hit the road – *Goodbye Horses* by Q Lazzarus – Kavitha ran at a good, even pace. She took her usual route, from East Capitol and 9th Street, S.E., to East Capitol and 3rd Street, past the Folger Shakespeare Library, the Jefferson Building of the Library of Congress, the Supreme Court, and the U.S. Capitol, down to 3rd Street and Madison Drive, S.W., on the National Mall, and back to Norman's house via the same route. But today, she sensed that she was being followed, so when she reversed her course, Annie Lennox belting out *Walking on Broken Glass*, she decided to run up the Capitol steps and back down before resuming her return route.

Back at 2nd and East Capitol Streets, S.E., she removed her earbuds and ran up the front steps to the west side of the Folger Library and ducked inside.

Special Police Officer John Morris was at the front desk. He recognized her, of course, and had no problem with her story about needing to use the restroom before continuing her run. "I like the ladies room downstairs," she told him. "I'll leave through the back door when I'm done."

"Sure, you can exit through Door 21," Officer Morris said.

Kavitha ran downstairs to the basement, past the restrooms, and directly to Door 21. She opened the door and ran through the alley between the Folger Library and the John Adams Building of the Library of Congress. She dashed past the U.S. Capitol Police guard booth, where officers controlled access to the John Adams Building's parking lot and past 3rd Street, down A Street, S.E., which runs parallel to East Capitol Street. She ran past 4th Street, S.E., past 5th Street, past 6th Street, to 7th Street, where she turned left and ran back to East Capitol, where she turned right. That's where she saw the black limousine parked on East Capitol Street, S.E. And then its rear passenger window rolled down to reveal the face of a man whom she'd presumed was dead by now.

"Please join me, Dr. Netram," said Rupert Whyte.

He opened the door and Kavitha climbed in and sat opposite him.

A block away on East Capitol at 6th Street, S.E., Afshar Ansary sat behind the wheel of a parked gray Mazda 3 rental car and watched Kavitha climb into the back of Rupert Whyte's limo. His operatives had informed him where Rupert was staying and he had followed Whyte himself this morning, from Linnean Avenue, N.W., to here. Dr. Netram was Rupert's go-to girl, he knew, and he wondered what caper they were working now, in league with that Folger Library security guard.

ABOUT THE AUTHOR

Quintin Peterson is the author of several plays and screenplays. He is a native Washingtonian.

As a junior high school student, he attended the Corcoran School of Art on a scholarship. While still in high school, he was honored with the University of Wisconsin's Science Fiction Writing Award, the National Council of Teachers of English Writing Award, and the Wisconsin Junior Academy's Writing Achievement Award.

As an undergraduate communications major at the University of Wisconsin, he wrote and performed in two plays for stage and videotape and received a Mary Roberts Rinehart Foundation grant for his play project, Change. A National Endowment for the Arts creative writing fellowship and a playwriting grant from the DC Commission on the Arts and Humanities followed. Subsequently, two of his radio plays were aired on WPFW-FM Pacifica Radio as productions of the Minority Arts Ensemble's Radio Drama Workshop '79.

Mr. Peterson was a police officer with the Metropolitan Police Department of Washington, D.C., for three decades, where he served for many years as media liaison officer and as the liaison between the department and members of the motion picture and television industries, acting as a script consultant and technical adviser. He also wrote and narrated training films for the police department. In December of 2010, he became an employee of the Folger Shakespeare Library's Department of Safety and Security.

An Active Member of Mystery Writers of America, Police Writers, and the Public Safety Writers Association (PSWA), he is the author of a book of poetry, **Nativity**; two crime novels, **SIN** and **The Wages of SIN**; is a contributor to six anthologies, *D.C. Noir*, edited by George Pelecanos, *Bad Cop, No Donut*, edited by John L. French; *From Shadows and Nightmares*, edited by Amber L. Campbell; *To Hell in a Fast Car*, edited by John L. French, *Felons, Flames and Ambulance Rides*, edited by Marilyn Olsen, and *Explosions: Stories of Our Landmined World*, edited by Scott Bradley; and has penned several e-stories available via Amazon Kindle and Barnes & Noble Nook Books. His short stories are also featured in the British horror magazine **SANITARIUM** and *Heater* (formerly *eNoir*) Magazine. A short story version of his novella, *Guarding Shakespeare* is featured in *eNoir (Heater)* Issue No. 2.

Made in the USA
Columbia, SC
11 May 2017